"As your e[mployer,]
patronizingly, "and the father of
your unborn child, I *insist* you stay
off work until you have your health
in order. *Then* we will discuss if and
where you can work."

Oh, he was smug over that.

"I'll make my own decisions, thank you very much."

"Then make smart ones!" He opened the door.

"How does quitting my job and moving in with you serve me in any way?"

"We just agreed we're doing this together." He nodded at her middle. "How does that happen if I'm in Barcelona and you're here? Because as soon as this acquisition is finalized, I'm finding a new CEO for LVG and will only be here quarterly."

"And you expect me to pick up sticks and go to Barcelona with you? For how long?"

"Twenty years?" he shrugged.

"You're unbelievable."

The driver arrived at the curb as they exited the building. Siobhan got into the car because she had a feeling Joaquin would have the driver take him to her building regardless.

Canadian **Dani Collins** knew in high school that she wanted to write romance for a living. Twenty-five years later, after marrying her high school sweetheart, having two kids with him, working at several generic office jobs and submitting countless manuscripts, she got The Call. Her first Harlequin novel won the Reviewers' Choice Award for Best First in Series from *RT Book Reviews*. She now works in her own office, writing romance.

Books by Dani Collins

Harlequin Presents

Awakened on Her Royal Wedding Night
Marrying the Enemy
Husband for the Holidays
His Highness's Hidden Heir
Maid to Marry
Hidden Heir, Italian Wife
The Greek's Wife Returns

The Sauveterre Siblings

Pursued by the Desert Prince
His Mistress with Two Secrets
Bound by the Millionaire's Ring
Prince's Son of Scandal

Diamonds of the Rich and Famous

Her Billion-Dollar Bump

Visit the Author Profile page
at Harlequin.com for more titles.

BOSS'S CHRISTMAS BABY ACQUISITION

DANI COLLINS

Harlequin
PRESENTS

If you purchased this book without a cover you should be aware that this book is stolen property. It was reported as "unsold and destroyed" to the publisher, and neither the author nor the publisher has received any payment for this "stripped book."

MIX
Paper | Supporting responsible forestry
FSC® C021394
www.fsc.org

Harlequin® PRESENTS™

ISBN-13: 978-1-335-21333-4

Boss's Christmas Baby Acquisition

Copyright © 2025 by Dani Collins

All rights reserved. No part of this book may be used or reproduced in any manner whatsoever without written permission.

Without limiting the author's and publisher's exclusive rights, any unauthorized use of this publication to train generative artificial intelligence (AI) technologies is expressly prohibited.

This is a work of fiction. Names, characters, places and incidents are either the product of the author's imagination or are used fictitiously. Any resemblance to actual persons, living or dead, businesses, companies, events or locales is entirely coincidental.

For questions and comments about the quality of this book, please contact us at CustomerService@Harlequin.com.

TM and ® are trademarks of Harlequin Enterprises ULC.

Harlequin Enterprises ULC
22 Adelaide St. West, 41st Floor
Toronto, Ontario M5H 4E3, Canada
www.Harlequin.com

HarperCollins Publishers
Macken House, 39/40 Mayor Street Upper,
Dublin 1, D01 C9W8, Ireland
www.HarperCollins.com

Recycling programs for this product may not exist in your area.

Printed in Lithuania

BOSS'S CHRISTMAS BABY ACQUISITION

A big thank you to Allie, a lovely fan who suggested I revisit The Sauveterre Siblings. I hope you enjoy this little catch-up with all of them.

CHAPTER ONE

Siobhan Upton hit the call button for the elevator then tapped to check her phone.

Ugh. Her sister was asking about Christmas. Again.

Siobhan was the youngest of four girls. Both her middle sisters had invited her to stay in America for Thanksgiving, a holiday they'd both adopted since moving here from London. Their mother was flying to Miami to stay with them and swore she wasn't leaving until winter was over back home.

Meanwhile, Siobhan's eldest sister, Cinnia, was pressuring her to spend Christmas with her and her family in Spain. Cinnia was hosting all her in-laws for the first time in years. Siobhan knew them well and genuinely loved them, especially the children, but she hadn't been able to enjoy Christmas since her bat guano of an ex-boyfriend had ruined that time of year for her five years ago.

She was dodging all of it by claiming to be focused on finding a job and a place to live. Which was true. She had these interviews in San Francisco then needed to get back to Sydney to pack up her flat, not sure where she would end up—

Wait.

She gasped with excitement as she saw the email from the placement agency.

Pleased to inform you... Employment contract will be forwarded... Expect you in Madrid on Monday December first...

"Yes!" That was only ten days away, but Siobhan punched the air and nearly leaped out of her borrowed Jimmy Choo heels.

"Are you going up?" The deep male voice held a hint of a Spanish accent.

She glanced up to see a man inside the elevator, holding the door for her.

Her heart took a swerve. Wow. He was really hot.

"Yes." She swallowed. "Thanks."

She stepped in beside him, blood fizzing for another reason. She tried not to stare, but he was kind of dazzling. He was thirty-ish and had an aura of dark sexiness with his thick black hair swept back from his forehead, and irises that were such a dark brown they seemed black. His cheeks were long and clean-shaven, his jaw well-defined. His nose was blade-sharp and his upper lip distinctly peaked.

As a uni student, Siobhan had fallen into wearing off-the-rack hoodies and other casual wear that helped her blend in, but she'd been around enough haute couture to recognize that navy suit was bespoke. It sat perfectly against his upper body, accentuating his broad shoulders and extremely fit physique.

Was he an actor? This was San Francisco, not LA, but he could be here on movie business. He certainly looked as though he financed blockbuster productions. Or starred in steamy thrillers as a morally gray character.

One thick black brow quirked, polite but patronizing. "Floor?"

"Oh, um..." Good grief, she was behaving like an idiot. As she tried to open the app, she watched him use his phone on the reader, then touch P. "That works for me. Thanks. I got the job I wanted." She wiggled her own phone as the doors closed. "I'm not usually such a scatterbrain."

"Congratulations."

"On not being a scatterbrain? Thanks."

The corner of his mouth twitched. "Australian?" he guessed.

"English. But I've been in Sydney long enough to adopt their accent." The better to blend in and not have her past follow her.

He was looking at her as though trying to make up his mind about something.

She warmed under his study, wondering when she'd last felt this level of instant attraction. Had she ever?

The doors opened to the foyer of the elite level. In front of her was a frosted door labeled Concierge. A fountain trickled a soothing rhythm next to a courtesy bench.

"Have a nice evening." Siobhan flashed a smile. She felt awkward as she turned away, as though she'd forgotten how to walk.

"Are you going to celebrate?" he asked behind her.

"I should, shouldn't I?" She experienced a rush of relief and pivoted to face him, then tilted her head as she considered it. "I have another interview tomorrow, but now that I've got the job I want, that's just for practice. Maybe I'll order champagne. My sister's paying for the room. Why not?" she added with a cheeky grin.

"No one to celebrate with? I'll buy you a drink." He nodded toward the private lounge reserved for guests on this floor.

Her inner defenses reflexively ran through her mental house, bolting and locking all the doors and windows. It was a PTSD response, not because she feared men. She was more than capable of taking care of herself on a physical level, but she didn't want to be used and betrayed again.

Even if he knew who she was, he didn't look like someone who needed her connections, though. *Did* he know who she was?

"You're not single?" He misinterpreted her hesitation. The hint of warmth in his expression turned to cool dismissal. "Perhaps another time."

"No, I am. I just..." *Never hook up.*

Not that she was thinking about *that*. She barely dated or even went out with friends. Her mates at school had been her age, but infinitely less mature and jaded. They had partied as often as they studied while Siobhan had focused on keeping a low profile and finally completing her degree. Her social life was mostly confined to family and conducted out of the public eye. Her trust in strangers was very low.

This particular stranger was exceedingly compelling, however. And she didn't want to drink her champagne in a hotel room while talking to her mother over the tablet. She wanted a few more minutes with him.

"I was just surprised," she said with a smile that felt unsteady.

"That a man offered to buy you a drink?" His black brows lifted in skepticism.

"No." A man at LaGuardia had offered to buy her a drink and there'd been a whole convention of men at the hotel in Miami trying to hit on her. "That I want to accept."

"Ah." His eyes narrowed slightly. She suspected that was as close as he got to a smile.

He was ringless, but she cocked her head to ask, "Are *you* single?"

"*Sí*. Joaquin." He offered his hand.

"Siobhan." She shook his hand and felt the tingle all the way up her arm.

Breathless, she walked into the empty lounge and excused herself to the powder room where she washed her hands and touched up her makeup, smoothing her brunette hair back into its chignon.

When she returned, Joaquin was at a table by the windows. He rose to help her with her chair. "The wind might break up the clouds and give us a sunset."

"It's a nice view either way." It was overcast and spitting rain, but the Golden Gate Bridge stood reddish-orange against the mist.

"Have you been here before?" he asked.

"No. And I leave after my interview in the morning so I won't have time to explore." She was looking for a menu, but the server arrived with an ice bucket and showed Joaquin a bottle of Cristal. He nodded for it to be opened.

"You're spoiling me," Siobhan said. "I would have ordered a split of the California bubbly."

"My family has vineyards. I'm a snob."

"Is that what brings you here? Are they here?"

"No, I had meetings. I'm in tech, heading to Asia tomorrow."

She suspected that was a deliberate detail to let her know this was a very casual encounter, barely a date, not the beginning of anything serious.

"Where do you live?" she asked curiously.

"These days? On my plane," he said ironically.

The cork popped. Joaquin smelled and tasted, then nodded his approval.

The server poured into a crystal flute rimmed in gold and offered it to her.

The pale amber sparkled with fine bubbles. Siobhan lifted it and closed her eyes as she inhaled the aroma of sea air and lime zest.

When the server walked away away, Joaquin said, *"Salud,"* and offered his glass.

"Cheers. And thank you." She touched her glass to his, then sipped. The delicate effervescence coated her tongue with a silky mousse-like texture. Buttery flavors of crushed nuts and yeasty sourdough melted in her mouth, followed by saline and citrus and a lengthy floral finish.

"You're also a snob," he accused lightly.

She opened her eyes to realize he'd watched her savor her first taste. Her heart hiccupped and her gaze got all tangled up in his intense stare. She licked her lips and his attention dropped to her mouth, making her pulse swerve again.

"I'm lucky enough to have been around the finer things in life." She lifted the glass. "I make the most of it when I can."

His brows went up in a prompt for more information.

"I'm not an escort," she blurted, suddenly fearing that was why he'd offered to buy her this drink.

"I didn't think you were." He was definitely laughing at her behind that impassive expression. "Tell me about your new job."

"I would, but then I'd have to kill you."

His dark gaze flickered to her shoulders and the slender wrist holding the delicate glass. "You could try."

"Don't be fooled. I've taken self-defense. I'm actually very dangerous."

"That, I believe." His expression was relaxed and she had his full attention. It was heady. A glow of enjoyment spread through her chest.

"I'm trying to sound more exciting than I am," she admitted. "The truth is I recently finished my BBA. I want to go into contract law, so I'm gaining experience in that field."

"How old does that make you?" His brows lowered into a frown.

"Relax. I'm twenty-four. Old enough to drink." And do other things. She bit back a smirk.

He made a noise of contemplation, and his gaze traveled over her short jacket and the dark hair gathered into the roll at her nape. "I couldn't tell. You look young, but you seem very self-possessed."

"Mature for my age?" she asked drily. "I've been told that all my life. Forty at fourteen."

"Are you still speaking to the people who said that?"

"Ha. Yes. Because they weren't wrong." She shrugged. "I was in such a hurry to grow up, I finished my A levels at sixteen by home study. Regular school was too slow and boring." And she had been helping Cinnia with her twins.

"Then what? You moved to Australia? Took a gap year?" His brows came together in calculation. "Or three?"

"I actually had most of a language degree completed by nineteen, but my education was interrupted." Thanks to that absolute turd weasel, Gilbert. She washed away the bitterness on her tongue. "I started over when I moved to Australia. Transferring the credits wasn't an option, but I still managed to finish early. I would have preferred to be further ahead by now, but…" She had needed to lick her wounds. Be someone else. Someone who didn't make stupid mistakes.

"Is this new job articling?"

"No. That's what I should be doing, but I'm sick of school." She rolled the stem of her glass between her finger and thumb. "This is just a maternity cover as an EA, but it's a good opportunity and puts me back into the real world. Plus, I'll be closer to my sister and her children. They're growing fast—" She stopped herself from prattling. "This is the real reason I didn't want to tell you about it. It makes me sound very dull."

"It could all be a lie to disguise the fact you're really an assassin." The corner of his mouth dug in before he hid the faint smile behind his glass.

"True. Siobhan isn't even my real name." She waved a dismissive hand. "That's both a joke and the truth. Siobhan is my second name."

"What's your first name?"

She wrinkled her nose in reluctance. "I don't share it. Not because I don't like it. I was named for my great-grandmother and I don't mind keeping her alive in that small way."

Her name was Doreena. Siobhan had grown up as Dorry. Her family still called her that, but hearing it was something she both loved and hated. It made her feel connected to them, but it was an uncomfortable reminder of that silly girl who had screwed up so badly.

"I just prefer Siobhan." Siobhan had her act together. Siobhan didn't make dangerous mistakes.

"Here I thought you were going to admit to hiding from the law."

"I love that you think I'm that interesting. No, the bald truth is I'm related by marriage to some very rich people." She watched him, looking for signs he already knew, but only saw mild curiosity in his expression. "That's how I can tell Cristal from Dom." She tilted her glass. "I was stung by someone who used me to get close to them so I changed my name to distance myself."

That was a very watered-down version. It was also a warning that she wouldn't allow it to happen again.

Anyone else would have asked: *Who are they?*

Joaquin gave an impassive blink. "Why contract law?"

"Are you suffering insomnia and need something to put you to sleep? Why are we still talking about *me*?"

"I'm interested."

Was he? He was listening attentively, but his motives were impossible to read. He was most likely trying to get lucky. Perhaps he was lonely. Maybe *he* was an assassin trying to blend in by having a drink with a stranger.

She really wanted to take him at his word, though. She was feeling a deep pull of attraction and yearned for it to be mutual.

"It's another deeply unsexy answer," she warned. "When I was young, our family went through some hard times. One of my sisters got into estate law to pay the bills. Probate and such."

"Not the direction desperate women usually take," he noted with a twitch of his lips.

"Right?" Siobhan grinned, but the truth was Cinnia had also been the girlfriend of a very rich man and had taken flack for it, even though that wasn't how she'd kept their family afloat. "She always said there was good money in doing the tedious work no one else wants to do. I have a good memory and I read fast. I'm detail-oriented and I can be cutthroat when necessary. I love the idea of achieving something difficult by wielding fine print."

"This is the sister who paid for your room?"

"No. I have three. The one who booked the room is married to a pro athlete. She travels with her husband and collects tons of points so she didn't technically pay for it. This—" Siobhan indicated the designer jacket she wore over a snug cashmere sweater and pleated trousers "—I stole from another sister's closet. She works in fashion. I take what fits and hope she doesn't notice."

"Ah. You're not hiding from the law. You're hiding from *her*," he accused.

"Truth. She's vicious when crossed."

"Are they all in Australia?"

"No, we're sprinkled everywhere." This was getting too personal so she turned it around. "What about you? Siblings? Any crimes against them you'd like to confess?"

His expression lost all its ease. His gaze dropped to the glass he was pinching.

"I had a brother. He passed eighteen months ago."

"I'm so sorry."

"You didn't know." He took a hefty gulp of champagne. "We'd grown apart. Things were complicated." His expression shuttered and he looked out the window. "I feel strongly that I let him down so yes, in that way I committed a crime of negligence that I'm trying to make up for with his children."

Oh. She understood that need to self-flagellate far too well. She couldn't help reaching across to set her hand on his hard wrist, offering what little compassion she could.

"It's so easy to believe there will be ample time later, isn't it? You don't have to talk about him if you don't want to, but you can. I understand *complicated* very well."

His gaze came up from where she touched his wrist. For a few seconds, she saw into his soul, where regret and glimmering coals of self-directed anger lived.

She felt the walls within her shift. They didn't fall

open, but they angled as though adjusting to nest against his. It became a shared beveled wall. It was the sensation of sitting back-to-back with someone. Not aligned, exactly, but occupying the same space.

He is *lonely*.

His hand shifted to take hold of hers and the mood altered again. Excitement flared within her, shocking in its intensity. There was a reciprocal flash in his eyes, one that made her skin burn where his thumb stroked across the backs of her knuckles.

"Let's talk about something else," he said.

"Something simple?" she suggested shakily, not moving her hand but very, very aware of how her fingers twitched in his loose grip. "Quantum mechanics, perhaps? Or fate versus free will?"

His mouth pulled sideways. "I lean heavily toward free will. You wouldn't have got the job you wanted if you hadn't applied. You wouldn't be having a drink with me if I hadn't invited you. You sat down because you wanted to." His thumb skimmed across her skin again, short-circuiting her brain.

"But you wouldn't have asked if we hadn't wound up in the same elevator," she challenged shakily. "Perhaps that was kismet."

"Please," he scoffed in that sinfully sexy accent of his. "I took one look at the attractive woman beside me and made a deliberate decision to shirk the calls I ought to be making."

"Say more." She was trying to hide that she was barely able to breathe under the lazy way he scanned her features. "I'm the mousy one so I'm usually overlooked."

"Who are you comparing yourself to? Your sisters?" He shook his head in refutation, fingers shifting to twine with hers in a way that felt very intimate. Now his thumb stroked at the base of her thumb into her inner wrist. It was deeply distracting. Arousing.

"How…um… How would you know?" Her suspicions reared. "Have you met them?"

"No." There was no subterfuge in his expression as he continued making love to her hand with his innocuous touch, sending signals into her chest that made her breasts tingle. "But I can't imagine there's any way to improve on perfection."

A bubble of incredulous laughter escaped her. She flushed with pleasure, though. "Your efforts to seduce me are working."

"I prefer to think of it as an invitation. It's up to you whether you accept. Free will and all that." He shifted his glass aside so he could use his other hand to reach across and brush a loose tendril of hair behind her ear. His fingertip caressed her ear and the edge of her jaw. "Would you like to order something to eat? Before we get drunk on champagne?"

"And each other?" It was a corny thing to say, but in her case, it was becoming all too true. She was losing her appetite for food and was no longer thirsty for champagne. She was falling into lust for the first time in her life.

"Mmm," he agreed in a rumble. "You're certainly intoxicating." He brought her hand to his mouth and nuzzled his lips into her palm.

Every bone in her body melted.

This wasn't the adolescent inquisitiveness that had driven her to kiss boys who were nothing but bravado and hormones. It wasn't the romantic infatuation that had drawn her into the bed of a dishonest man. This was something exciting and enthralling. A pull that was filled with promise. With *need*.

She had agreed to have a drink in a seize-the-day impulse. It was another step toward coming out of her self-imposed exile. She had already been high on being chosen for her merit, not her connections. This was another octave of that. He knew nothing about her except what she'd told him. It felt good to be desired purely for herself.

It felt good to *feel*. For the first time in a long time, the numbness of betrayal was falling away. She felt feminine and desirable and brimming with her own sexual power. She felt like indulging herself.

"Why don't we take the champagne to your room?" Her voice thickened with a mixture of shyness and the eroticism that was taking her over. "We can order food later."

"That is an act of free will I can get behind." He kept her hand as he rose and drew her from her chair.

CHAPTER TWO

Joaquin Valezquez didn't make a habit of picking up women. Which wasn't to say it had never happened, but he was a busy man who couldn't afford distractions, especially today.

Thirty minutes ago, word of yet another one of his father's financial overextensions had reached him. Joaquin had left his team finishing out his presentation to a tech mogul and called his father on his way to the hotel. Just hearing Lorenzo's voice made his skin crawl. Trying to work *with* him was like trying to reason with a swarm of murder hornets. Every time Joaquin swatted at one damaging sting, another threatened from a new direction. Nothing about it was pain-free.

Brooding on the fact he had to find a more permanent way to keep his father from destroying the legacy that belonged to his brother's children, Joaquin had stepped into the elevator that opened as he arrived in front of it.

His mind had been on the calls he had to make. The plans that needed hammering out. There had been rumbles among the board of LV Global that they would be willing to vote Lorenzo out if Joaquin stepped in as CEO.

Joaquin would rather go back to scrubbing toilets for

drunk tourists than take over LVG, but someone had to. He needed to call a headhunter and his sister-in-law. Others.

Despite his preoccupation, his libido had absolutely noticed the woman who seemed to be waiting for the elevator. She was well dressed in a casually tasteful way. Her smart jacket and designer trousers made the most of her figure without being blatant about it. She struck him as a sophisticated woman who was establishing herself in a professional field. Her dark brown hair was in a tidy roll at her nape. Her profile was a graceful line that belonged on the kind of pink brooch his grandmother had once worn.

When a huge smile arrived on her face, she was incandescent.

His cloud of distemper had lifted. He asked if she was going up.

She met his gaze and his breath stopped. She was genuinely beautiful. Her makeup enhanced a wide mouth and high cheekbones and long brows that delivered an impression of intelligence and directness. Confidence.

As she looked at him, her bright blue eyes took on a gleam of interest that was deeply gratifying when he was in such a foul mood.

She'd said something funny as she joined him. He'd already forgotten what it was because she seemed to offer a lot of throwaway remarks that kept him on his toes.

Siobhan. Her name was as charming as the rest of her. She seemed both open and closed, playful yet careful. Empathetic without offering pity. She was lovely to look at and sensual in the way she appreciated her first taste of wine. When he took her hand, her pulse skipped under his touch.

That had been as enticing as a flick of a ribbon to the desire prowling like a jungle cat inside him. He was wound up and longing for a chase and a capture and a wrestle.

As he opened the door of his suite for her, she carried their half-full glasses inside, offering him a whiff of vanilla and oranges from her hair as she passed.

He let the door fall closed and set the ice bucket on the coffee table, then dropped his phone beside it. He joined her at the window and took back his glass.

"Have you ever been to Alcatraz?" She nodded at the view through the shroud of the curtain and the mist on the water.

Metaphorically, he'd grown up there. "No."

She slid a sideways look at him and seemed to grow skittish, putting a few steps between them. "I want you to know that I never do this."

The loping animal in him slowed his pace. "When you say *never*..."

Her chin dipped coyly. "I'm not a virgin. I mean I don't jump into bed with strangers."

Her cheeks flushed pink. She was trying to be bold, but she was shy at heart. Fascinating.

"I'm not making judgments. Or assumptions." After a beat, he magnanimously added, "We don't have to use the bed. Lady's choice."

Her throaty laughter was as much a turn-on as the rest of her, filling the room with her presence. "Good to know. That helps my nerves a lot. Thanks."

"This is you nervous?" She had invited herself in here! "God help the man who encounters you when you're feeling confident."

Her mouth pulled wide in a satisfied show of her teeth. "Thank you for that. I actually hate feeling less than five thousand percent confident. But you've got all of this going on..." She motioned at him in an encompassing way. "It's intimidating."

"I think there might be a compliment buried in there," he said drily. "But to be clear, I like five thousand percent consent. If you're here because you feel intimidated, or you think I expect sex because I bought you a glass of champagne, then we need a longer conversation before we do anything else."

"That's not what I think. I'm very comfortable saying no when I need to. I've made a habit of it for a while now." Her mouth twisted with irony. "More often than I needed to. It's the saying yes that makes me feel out of my depth. I'm out of practice."

"Like saying yes to a drink?"

"Exactly. I don't know how to be spontaneous anymore, but I'd like to be. If you're getting mixed signals, that's why."

"You use truth to disarm," he replied, studying that contradiction of squared shoulders and a high chin with the pink that sat in her cheeks and the way her lashes kept screening her thoughts. "You only reveal a sliver of the truth, though. It's a clever sleight of hand."

"Is that a compliment?" Her brows went up to a haughty level as she mocked him with his own words. "Because you've buried it."

"I believe you're nervous." Even though she was disguising it well. "I'm observing how well you counteract it by calling it out. The way you're confiding in me sounds like a sign of trust, but it also lets me know I can't take advantage of you. Not if we're being honest with each other."

"You're making it sound like I came in here to screw with your mind not your body. I assure you it's the latter."

"Please continue with both. As foreplay goes, I'm enjoying it." He swirled the final mouthful of champagne in the bottom of his glass before swallowing it, meeting her gaze over the disc of the stem.

Her blue eyes glittered with amusement.

Dios, she was marvelous. He hadn't even kissed her yet and he wanted weeks and months and years to saturate himself in her.

That thought brought him up short. He had a few hours. The night at best. The slow-motion train wreck in Madrid needed mitigating. Dealing with his father required all of his concentration and a matching level of ruthlessness.

Joaquin loathed the idea of being anything like his father. It made him sick to contemplate it so he brushed that disturbing prospect aside. He set down his glass and ambled toward Siobhan, watching her eyes widen.

"There's no rush," he assured her. "No signed contract to fulfill. Leave anytime. But I'm dying to kiss you." He cupped the side of her neck and gave her a beat to decide.

Her gaze held his until her pupils expanded, then her lashes swept down. Her attention dropped to his mouth and her lips parted in tremulous invitation.

"I want that, too." She leaned into him, mouth up-tilted in offering.

He sealed his lips over hers and desire exploded within him.

Yes. Here was the portal to escape he'd been looking for.

Siobhan hadn't realized what a sense of heightened anticipation she'd been in until his mouth covered hers and relief arced through her.

There were still nervous crackles in the back of her mind. What if he was an accomplished liar? What if it wasn't *her* he wanted, but *them*?

All of that receded behind the avalanche of more immediate signals—the lingering taste of champagne on his tongue, the subtle notes of aftershave applied hours ago against skin that was warm with the musk of his own personal scent. The lightest scuff on his chin where his five o'clock stubble was coming in. The seductive play of his fingertips against her neck, masterful as a pianist teasing a love song from his keys.

A moan of need left her. She flowed into him, arms lifting to twine around his neck.

His arm twitched and there was a delicate ping and shatter of crystal against tile.

He broke their kiss and they both looked down at the glass she'd dropped.

In the next second, his arms slid around her. He lifted her off her feet and pivoted her out of the broken shards. As he set her back down, his mouth captured hers again, eclipsing all but the heavenly feel of him firmly surrounding her. Strong, restless hands slid under the back of her jacket, pressing her closer. He angled his head to kiss her deeper. She tightened her arms around his neck to arch herself into the bow of his towering frame.

All she knew was the erratic pulse in her ears, the sear of sexual heat in her blood, the edgy hunger that wanted to *devour* him. She slid her hands into his hair and lightly scraped her nails against his scalp.

The sound he made was regressive and thrilling. In a powerful move, he swept her up into the cradle of his arms. His gaze tracked over her with possessive satisfaction before coming back to meet hers, flashing with demand.

She was still trying to catch her breath. A fine tremble weakened her muscles. She suddenly had a new appreciation for how powerful he was. How unknown. Nerves accosted her again. Apprehension paired with a thrill of excitement.

"Say yes," he commanded.

Oddly, his stern demand was the reassurance she needed. He wouldn't do anything she didn't want. But she did want. Her desire for him was profound.

Holding his intent stare, she toed off one shoe, letting it thud to the floor. Then the other. Her sister would kill her for treating them so poorly, but the way his nostrils flared was worth it.

"Quit being a brat."

She curled her arms around his neck and pressed her smile into his throat, then licked the salty skin near his Adam's apple. "*Sí.* Take me to your bed, Joaquin."

He hitched her a little higher and carried her into the

bedroom where he set her on her feet. "You're too short now," he grumbled.

She moved to kneel on the edge of the bed. "Better?"

"Much." He aligned himself against her and they kissed again, brushing each other's jackets away. "I could pet you for days in this," he said of her cashmere sweater, hands skimming deliciously over her shoulders and back and rib cage and breasts.

For a long time, that was all he did. He petted and kissed her until she was leaning off the edge of the mattress, trying to get closer to him. Seeking the ridge of flesh that she wanted to feel in the cradle of her thighs.

"Wait here." He steadied her before he walked into the bathroom.

She sat back on her heels, trying to blink herself out of the fog of arousal and the sudden denial of his touch. It could have been a moment to catch her bearings and rethink this, but he was already coming back.

He threw a strip of condoms onto the bed. "I presume I need those."

"You do." She was thrown by how little thought she'd given to protection, but she wasn't on the pill anymore.

He began undressing so she did the same, tilting up the edge of her sweater to ask, "May I? Or did you want me to keep it on?"

"You may." He granted his permission in a deep tone of authority that should have made her balk. He wasn't the boss of her, but that hint of dominance was kind of a turn-on.

He wanted to control this moment and she wanted to push back so she took her time peeling up the edge of the ultra-soft knit, revealing one centimeter of skin at a time, stretching tall and holding her arms up to give him a long look at the demicups made from blue-and-gold lace that she wore beneath it.

"You very much may," he said in a pleased rumble as he pulled the sweater free of her upraised arms and discarded it on the floor. "*Dios*, that's pretty." He traced the edge of the lace along the upper swell of her breast, tickling her skin.

Her nipple peaked against silk. He took care to reward her response with a lingering caress there.

"Take your hair down," he said as he brought both his hands into play against the bra cups.

He was shirtless now and her hands went to his naked shoulders, wanting to feel all of his satiny skin. Wanting to kiss him and taste the hot plane of his chest.

He dragged her hands from his neck and moved them to the back of her head. "Let me see how long it is," he insisted.

A helpless protest throbbed in her throat, but she did as he asked, pulling pins that fell willy-nilly to the floor.

As she did, he steadied her with his hands on her waist, watching intently. When the brunette waves fell around her shoulders, he ran his fingers through the length and held her head for a long, hot, ravenous kiss.

She was so lost in that dark, velvety space, she didn't realize the weight of his hand was tangled in her hair, tugging her head back until his lips moved into her throat and down. He brushed aside her locket and dislodged the cup of her bra, lifting her breast to capture her nipple with the pull of his mouth.

Lightning streaked into her loins. She clasped at his shoulders, thinking she was about to fall onto her back, but his arm slid to support her as he held her off balance and feasted on her breast, teasing and feeding those fingers of electric heat that lanced through her abdomen and detonated between her thighs.

When she thought she couldn't stand another moment of those intense sensations, of feeling suspended and helpless and consumed, he moved to her other breast.

"Joaquin," she panted, shaking with arousal. Her core was drowning in neglect.

He lifted his head. "Too hard? I want to eat you up."

"I want...*this*." She splayed her hand on his abdomen then slid her palm lower to cup the thick ridge behind his fly.

He yanked open his belt and unzipped. She slid her hand inside the heat, behind the waistband of his boxer briefs, and clasped the steely weight of his erection.

He groaned into her mouth as he kissed her again, letting her explore his shape, running his hands over her back and buttocks, nipping at her ear and tugging at her hair again until he made a rough noise of tested restraint and caught her wrist.

"Finish undressing."

She opened her trousers, then dropped onto her back to work them off her hips and down her legs. As she kicked them away, she arched to reach behind herself and release her bra.

She was still untangling herself from the bra straps when he pressed a hand to her hip, stilling her so he could study the panties that matched her bra.

"You have exquisite taste." He followed the lace across her hip and into the V it took over her mound.

She bit her lip. Dampness flooded into the flesh that he traced through silk.

"H-how would you know?" she asked in a wicked challenge that was pure audacity.

"Oh, I will find out. Trust me on that, *querida*." He peeled her panties down and away before he touched her again, this time letting his fingertip sink into the slippery folds that parted easily under his caress.

"Blond," he noted of the neatly trimmed thatch. His curious gaze came up to the hair she colored, but she wasn't capable of conversation. He had found her sweet spot and knew exactly how to incite the most delicious sensations.

She couldn't keep her eyes open. Climax gathered as tension in her abdomen. *Need.*

"I want to be inside you so badly, I can hardly breathe," he said in a rasp, gently invading with a wicked touch.

She stilled his hand. "I'm going to come," she gasped.

"Then you should." He pressed deeper and his thumb rolled across the knot of nerves that was already pulsing.

With a harsh groan, she pinned his hand with her own, thighs clamping closed while her body twisted in the throes of acute pleasure.

It should have been embarrassing to lose control with him watching in the full light of day, but it felt *so good*. Wave after wave rolled through her, each one more gratifying than the last, until she was shaken and breathless and floating.

As the storm receded, he eased his hand away and

nudged her thighs open, rolling her onto her back. Her heart was still galloping, her breasts quivering with her uneven breaths.

He finished stripping and kicked away his clothes, gloriously naked from powerful shoulders to defined abs to thrusting erection.

She blindly felt for the condoms and offered them.

"I have promises to keep, *querida*." His mouth slanted into a sinfully cruel smile and he bent to steal a wicked, intimate taste between her thighs.

She cried out. And shuddered with fresh longing. Then she moaned as he pulled her hips to the edge of the bed and mercilessly drew her back to a state of acute arousal. When her fists were in his hair and she was lifting her hips in a plea for the climax that hovered so elusively, he rose and reached for the condoms.

"As I said. Exquisite." His expression held carnal intent, but he said, "Now, tell me again what you want. Be specific."

"You. This." She caressed the naked column of heat as he moved her up the mattress and used his knee to spread her thighs. She squeezed and sought the places that made him twitch. She was completely stripped of inhibition. "I want to taste you." She licked her lips.

His breath huffed out as though he'd been punched.

"But I also want to feel you here." She ran her hand to her own sex, where she was soaked and aching.

"Then you shall have me," he said through his teeth and rolled on the condom.

As he loomed over her, she guided him into place. He

filled her in one firm, perfect thrust that made her arch in glorious abandon.

When he kissed her, she tasted herself and it only made the experience more erotic. Profound. She wrapped her arms and legs around him and urged him to unleash his full power, propelling them both into the volcano.

Coated in sweat and still suffering aftershocks from his powerful orgasm, Joaquin dragged himself free of her. He discarded the condom, then dropped onto his back beside her. His chest continued to heave, striving to catch his breath.

What had started as a pleasant diversion had turned into something that bordered on cataclysmic. Sex was supposed to be just sex. It was a shared experience in which he gave more than he took. He was never as generous with his business partners as his intimate ones, but in bed it was a case of wanting the same thing: pleasure. Giving was as good as getting for him. They were two sides of the same coin. The encounter was delightful while it lasted and afterward, his appetite was sated. His desire to possess was gone.

So why did he have this prickling sense of loss?

It wasn't the grief of losing his brother. Not the reduction of assets due to stock market fluctuations or other business cycles. This was the sense of something being *taken*. Held out of reach.

Which didn't make sense because she was right here.

And he had no intention of keeping her.

This unsettled sensation was a belated reaction to his father's attempts to manipulate him, he decided. He was stuck in the confluence of two crashing forces: his desire to expunge his father from his life and his responsibility to his brother's wife and children. He'd taken brief refuge from that mental war in the fleshy paradise that was Siobhan. He didn't regret it, but he couldn't let this respite she'd offered him become more significant than it was.

He couldn't let desire for her dull him to his duty.

"You know when you get a really great massage and you never want to move again?" She rolled onto her stomach and hugged the pillow that she pulled under her head and chest. Her eyelids drooped heavily as she blinked at him. The corners of her lips tilted in libidinous pleasure. "That's how I feel right now," she purred.

"I don't get those kinds of massages, but no judgment."

"As if!" Her teeth flashed and she slid across the sheet to drape herself over his chest, making him delightfully aware of the way her breasts brushed his skin before settling warm and plump against him. "I thought you promised me dinner?"

"Are you hungry? Why on earth would that be?" Despite his decision to distance himself, he absently gathered her more fully atop him. "I can order something. Or would you rather dress and go out?" Leaving this room would be prudent.

"This is nice." She shifted in a full body caress, legs interlacing with his own in a way that was pure seduction.

"It is." He ran his hands down her back and over the cool cheeks of her ass, thinking the cashmere had been lovely, but he preferred her naked skin. Perhaps he would indulge himself, and her, a little longer.

But only a little.

She nuzzled his jaw and her hair fell across his mouth. He brushed it back behind her ear.

"Why do you color it?" Not that he was complaining. On the contrary, he was mildly turned on by the fact *he* knew her natural color and few others did.

"No one takes me seriously as a blonde." She slid off him and sat up, letting her dark hair fall forward to curtain her profile. "Do you mind if I pop down to my room? I need to take out my contacts." She blinked at him.

He kept getting the sense she was hiding something. It provoked his frustration that he wouldn't get the chance to learn all her secrets, but such was his life right now.

He kept a light tone as he said, "If you come back and your eyes aren't blue, I really will believe you work for the government."

"But which one?" she challenged with a cheeky grin.

He slid his fingers along her hip and thigh, unable to keep from enjoying the supple softness of her. She was a warm, glowing light that mesmerized him the way a candle flame drew a moth.

"My eyes are blue. I promise." Her expression altered as she noticed the scar on the side of his chest. She gently traced it. "Broken rib? That was a bad one."

"It was," he agreed impassively, not telling her the hospital stay had been a relief from worse.

Her mouth grew pensive and her touch on that sensitive scar began to burn.

He caught her hand and carried it to his lips so he could kiss her palm.

She let him, but looked deeply into his eyes. "You don't want to talk about it."

"I don't." He tried to soften his words with a caress of her cheek, but he couldn't escape the fact he was setting hard, necessary boundaries. "If you're looking for someone you can truly share secrets with, I am not that man."

She blinked in a way that suggested his words had struck like a blow. She bit the corner of her mouth and looked toward the window as she sat up and withdrew her hand.

He fought the urge to drag her down into his arms again. To press her beneath him and make her his all over again. He'd never been possessive. He hadn't been allowed to be. Everything was Fernando's with very few crumbs left over for the spare.

Joaquin had taught himself *not* to want anything to be his. That had helped enormously when it came to gambling in tech manufacturing. He was willing to take risks that others weren't, simply because he didn't attach himself to material wealth or personal recognition. Losing a contract or a sum of money annoyed him, but he didn't let it affect him too deeply. The global company his father was now dangling like a carrot, pretending he had intentions of allowing Joaquin to run it? It meant absolutely nothing to him. He didn't want it. At all. Only his loyalty to his brother compelled him to take an interest in keeping it afloat.

Siobhan, though. He discovered he wanted Siobhan.

It was visceral, this urge to grasp onto her and keep her by his side.

Which was disturbing enough to prevent him from giving in to that desire. Everything he possessed needed to be something he was willing to lose. It was the only way to stay sane. Fear of losing something he really wanted was the reason he coveted nothing.

He tucked his arm beneath his head to keep from reaching for her, but his conscience pinched as he acknowledged she might not be as sophisticated as he'd judged her to be.

"I've hurt your feelings."

"No." He suspected she was saving face, adding with forced lightness, "Apparently, you're right about fate and free will. We're not meant to be. This was lovely, though. Thank you." Her hair spilled across his chest and cheek as she tapped his mouth with hers then flitted away just as quickly.

Was. He unwound his arm from behind his head, but she was already sliding off the bed. "You're not coming back?"

"You still want me to?" she asked over her shoulder, allowing him to glimpse a vulnerability in her gaze that kicked at his conscience again.

Let her go, he told himself, but his mouth said, "If you want to."

Her smile dawned in a way that expanded light inside him, promising a stay of execution from the mess that awaited in Madrid.

As she dressed, he rose to pull on his own trousers,

then followed her into the lounge where she picked up her shoes, but didn't put them on.

"My walk of shame is only down the hall."

"Is that how you feel?" he asked with dismay. "Ashamed?"

"No. I'm actually feeling very smug." She slid him a heavy-lashed look that tightened his skin.

"Good. I'll order dinner and call someone to clean up the glass. Hurry back."

They kissed lightly. Too lightly. If he'd known it would be their last kiss, he would have made it count.

CHAPTER THREE

Two weeks later...

SIOBHAN HAD BARELY learned how her new boss, Oladele, liked her coffee when she came in to find the woman already at her desk, still wearing a raincoat speckled with the drizzle of Madrid's December morning. Among the handful of people who had also trickled in before nine, there was an air of alertness. Something was going on. Something big.

Oladele was VP of Legal here at LV Global. She'd risen in the ranks under the previous president, Fernando Valezquez, and still choked up when she spoke of him. He'd passed suddenly over a year ago. It had been an electrical accident of some kind. His father, Lorenzo, had since come out of retirement to retake the helm.

"We're in a state of transition," Oladele had told Siobhan on her first day. "Señor Valezquez will return to retirement once a decision is made on his successor." Her expression had been pleasant, but as deadpan as a high-stakes poker player's.

Siobhan's antennae had gone up, thinking there was a lot that Oladele was leaving unsaid, but she wasn't likely to be forthcoming until Siobhan had proven herself trustworthy. Oladele had hired Siobhan for her legal aspirations, her fluency in six languages, including Modern Standard Arabic, her stellar grades and the security abstract she had voluntarily attached to her CV.

Siobhan had a feeling that last item had been the clincher because there seemed to be ample staff here at LV Global who could have stepped into the shoes of Oladele's very pregnant EA.

After two days of orientation with that EA, Siobhan was on her own. She loved everything about the job and the new life she was starting. She had leased a gorgeous one-bedroom flat in the barrio de Chamberí and, so far, was still unrecognized as Dorry Whitley. She would ride that horse as long as it had legs.

The only stitch in her side was the memory of returning to Joaquin's hotel room in San Francisco to find the door propped open. A young woman from housekeeping had been sweeping up the broken glass.

"He said to tell you he had to leave, but to charge your dinner to this room and take the champagne." The woman had pointed at the bottle in the bucket of melted ice.

Siobhan had stood there in a hotel robe over fresh lingerie that she had put on for *him*. She had felt so cheap, so scorned, so *foolish*, she had wanted to die.

She should have celebrated her new job alone, she kept telling herself. But that thought was always followed by a slithery reminder of how delicious the sex had been—which she almost wished had been terrible because now the bar had been set so high, she feared she was spoiled for anyone else.

Why were men so awful? Why was she so terrible at seeing how awful they were?

"I'll be right up," she heard Oladele say. The phone landed hard in its cradle.

Siobhan snapped out of her funk and finished removing her coat. She dropped her bag into its drawer and rushed into Oladele's office.

"Did I miss a text about an early meeting?" It was a mortifying thought. She prided herself on being thorough and prepared.

"I only learned an hour ago that there was an emergency board meeting." Oladele started to remove her coat and Siobhan hurried to help her. Oladele was a diminutive woman of fifty-three with narrow shoulders and a very short haircut, which formed a cap of tight curls against her scalp.

"I'll make your coffee. What else do you need? Did you miss breakfast?"

"I did, and yes to the coffee, but we're needed upstairs. Bring your laptop."

"May I ask what happened?"

"We're merging with another firm." Oladele flicked her gaze to the open door. "That's the language you will use," she added quietly with a warning tilt of her brows. "I didn't expect it to happen like this, definitely not this quickly, but here we are."

Siobhan didn't have time to process what that might mean. Within moments, they were hurrying off the elevator onto the top floor, which was the company president's domain.

She hadn't been up here yet. It was ten times more luxurious and imposing than the offices they occupied two floors below. The entire building was tastefully updated from the original construction a hundred years ago. Everything she'd seen was sophisticated and refined.

She had barely taken in the beautiful inlay of the mahogany and oak in the parquet floor, or the oval-shaped wall that separated the empty receptionist's desk from the rest of the floor, when the sound of an age-graveled baritone struck her ears.

"You thief! You think you can do this to me? You vile piece of—" An ugly streak of insults was hurled, growing loud enough to send a spike of alarm through Siobhan.

Another male voice responded, low and cold, saying something about protecting *it* for the children.

Shock waves went through her as she heard the second voice. It wasn't just the lethal tone. He almost sounded like—

No. She was imagining things. Joaquin was Spanish, but he wouldn't be *here*. That was too much of a bizarre coincidence.

In front of her, Oladele checked her step. Siobhan copied her, moving to set her back to the wall as a man with iron-gray hair strode with purpose toward them. His navy suit was well tailored to accommodate his barrel chest and stocky frame. His jaw wore a frost of stubble, as though he'd missed shaving this morning. His hair was slicked back, but untidy. His face was purple with fury.

He glared at Oladele as he passed them.

"Lorenzo," Oladele murmured, offering a deferential nod.

"You helped him, didn't you?" He was so livid, spittle had collected in the corners of his mouth. He glared blame at both of them. "Judas. I should have fired you when I had the chance. This is not over." He moved past them to jab the button for the elevator.

Oladele looked shaken, but motioned for Siobhan to accompany her into a foyer where a chandelier in a recessed ceiling hung over a small arrangement of late nineteenth century furniture. Three tall windows looked onto Madrid's business district. On another wall, shelves of old books were fronted by doors with paned glass.

"Wait here while I step into the meeting room. The board may still be in discussions." Oladele moved through a pair of open doors into a corridor.

Siobhan shifted to read a few titles on the books, which gave her a view down the hallway. She wasn't trying to spy, but she heard a door open and a woman's voice said in Spanish, "I should get back. The children will be awake and looking for me."

"Of course," a male voice replied. *That* male voice, the one that sent a preternatural shiver through Siobhan, making her abdomen clench and her scalp tighten.

She watched in mesmerized horror as a stunning woman stepped from the office at the end of the hall. The elegant brunette wore a wool skirt in gray plaid with a black turtleneck and a camel-colored overcoat. She was tying a green silk scarf over her hair.

Then *he* stepped out. Joaquin.

Siobhan's heart stopped. He was even more handsome than when she'd last seen him. The image of him shirtless, wearing only his trousers and a half-lidded look of satisfaction was imprinted on her mind. Today he had the air of a man who'd taken care with his appearance. He was shaved and had a fresh haircut. His somber blue suit fit him like armor, giving an impression he had dressed for an important moment. A ceremony.

Or a burial.

Her jumble of sensual memories collided with harsh reality, sending a piercing sensation through her belly, one that was steely and sharp and locked her in place.

Her morbid inability to look away meant she watched him bend his head to kiss both of the woman's cheeks with casual familiarity.

"My car should be waiting for you. I'll see you later—"

He spotted Siobhan and stood at attention. His glare of astonishment traveled down the length of the corridor like a quaking force, crashing into her and knocking her breath from her lungs.

"What are you doing here?" he demanded.

Her heart was already thudding in guilt and horror. Now adrenaline leaked into her blood, urging her to run, but she couldn't move. She was frozen in shock. In repulsion at him and herself.

He was *married*?

At that second, Oladele stepped from a door midway along the hall, arriving between them.

"Señor Valezquez," she said politely. "Señora. It's nice to see you." Oladele followed the stark glare Joaquin had pinned on Siobhan. "Ah. No need to be alarmed. Siobhan is covering my assistant's maternity leave. Siobhan, this is Joaquin Valezquez, our new president. Congratulations, señor."

Siobhan was probably expected to say something similar. Maybe, "It's nice to meet you." She couldn't speak. She wanted to die. She wanted to run from the building and never come back. She wanted to scream, *Married? You're married?*

"You have a busy day ahead. I'll leave you to it," the woman in the green scarf said. She offered Siobhan a curious smile as she left to go home to their *children*.

Oh, he was horrible. He was every bit as cold-blooded and manipulative as Gilbert in a completely different way. She was an *idiot*.

"Siobhan?" Oladele prompted. "I believe we're meeting in the president's office." She looked to Joaquin for confirmation.

"I just need..." She couldn't finish. Could barely speak. She dove through the door marked with the stenciled figure of a triangle with a dot on its point. Her behavior was deeply unprofessional, but this was a full-blown panic attack.

She had asked him if he was single and he had lied straight to her face before pulling her into an adulterous liaison.

Hot tears blinded her as she emptied her arms onto the vanity shelf beneath the mirror. She pushed into a stall where she leaned on the door, thinking she might throw up. She sat down, so lightheaded she was afraid she'd faint and knock herself cold on the porcelain.

* * *

"I—" Oladele sounded perplexed and took a step to follow Siobhan.

"When did you hire her?" Joaquin asked with acute suspicion, attention pinned to the lavatory door that had closed behind Siobhan.

"She started at the beginning of last week. Why? Do you know her?"

"I'm not sure," he lied. Hell, yes, he knew her. His body had recognized her with a pulse of animal lust the second he glimpsed her, roaring in a way that nearly overshadowed his astonishment at seeing her here of all places. "Can I see her file?"

"Her credentials are excellent. She's actually overqualified—"

He shot Oladele a look that had her pressing her lips into a line.

"But if that's something you would like to review yourself, I'll go to my desk and forward it," she said mildly. "I don't have access to those documents on my phone."

"Thank you."

At that moment, the board members began filing out of the meeting room.

Oladele moved into the sea of bodies flowing toward the elevator.

Still twitching with aggression from that volatile meeting, and now at this unexpected interloper, Joaquin kicked the stoppers out of the doors at the end of the corridor, closing it into privacy. Then he walked into the ladies' room, checked that there was only one pair of feet in the stalls, and turned the lock on the main door.

"Siobhan."

"What the hell?" The stall door clapped open. "You can't be in here."

She stepped out, pale face flushing red with high emotion, every bit as entincingly beautiful as he remembered.

He had to consciously keep his gaze from wandering to the open collar of her striped shirt and well-cut, single-button blazer. Her outfit was professional and conservative, exactly as it should be for her role as assistant to their head of legal.

He still found her entirely too sexy.

"I just acquired the building with the company." He leaned on the partition that separated the sink area from the vanity nook. "I can go anywhere I want. What are *you* doing here?"

"In this room?" She pointed to the floor. "Trying not to vomit over the fact that I slept with a married man. Who has *children*. You absolute disgusting scumbag. How *dare* you lie to me about something like that?"

Her anger was incendiary. Thrilling. She radiated the energy of a typhoon, terrifying yet awe-inspiring. There was also something perversely gratifying in her temper. She wasn't merely offended. *How dare you lie to* me. It was personal. She was jealous.

He shouldn't like that. At all. But he did.

"You're referring to Zurina?" He lifted one patronizing brow. "She's my sister-in-law."

"Oh." Her hard boil of fury simmered down to an

annoyed scowl. She narrowed her eyes on him, though. "You really aren't married? Because—"

"I am exactly as I presented to you when we met. You are the one with something to explain. How the hell do you come to be working for my father?" That was highly suspicious. *Highly.*

"I don't." She was taken aback. "I work for Oladele. Aside from when your father walked by us ten minutes ago, I'd never seen or spoken to him." She moved to the sink to wash her hands.

"You want me to believe your working here is a coincidence?"

"Unless *you* planned it, then yes. That's exactly what it is. I told you I was starting a new job covering a mat leave."

"You let me believe that was in Australia. Or San Francisco." He didn't know what he'd thought, but he sure as hell hadn't imagined she was coming *here*.

"You said you live on your *plane*. Maybe if you'd stuck around, instead of skittering away like a spider under a door, I would have told you I was coming to Madrid." She shook out a cloth hand towel and wet it under the tap. "You could have simply let me leave without asking me to come back. That second trip down the hall really was a walk of shame." She gave the wet towel a hard wring and dabbed a corner of it under her eyes, fixing her smudged makeup.

Tears? He might have been more disturbed by that if he wasn't seeing them here, amid an outright war with his father.

"Zurina called me with an emergency." He hadn't

liked leaving without a word, but he hadn't relished knocking on doors to find her, then trying to explain.

He hadn't liked that there'd been a part of him that had leaped toward asking her to accompany him. For that reason, a clean break had seemed easier. Safer.

But the clean break hadn't happened.

"Go back to explaining how you're here," he demanded.

"You really think I'm here by design? Until Oladele said it a few minutes ago, I didn't know your last name." She pivoted to face him, forcing him to quit ogling the shape of her ass in her blue trousers.

"You didn't investigate the company you were applying at?" he asked skeptically.

"I used a placement agency. They gave me an abstract, but I wasn't told it was LV Global until I'd been offered the job. I spoke to Oladele at one point, but that was about my duties. When I did look it up, it said the president had passed away over a year ago and that his father had come out of retirement to run things." She threw the damp towel in the laundry basket. "Frankly, I didn't need to know more than that. My priority was to be closer to my sister and gain experience in legal. I've been meaning to read more about the company, but I've been busy moving continents and visiting with family."

This all seemed too tidy for him to believe. On the other hand, there was very little on line that linked him to his father. He certainly didn't take any pains to acknowledge his relationship to Lorenzo.

She waved at the door. "Is Oladele out there, wondering why you're accosting her EA in the toilet?"

"She's downstairs." He stole a quick glance at his phone. The file hadn't been forwarded yet so they had another minute. "You can't work for me."

"I don't. I work for Oladele."

"She works for LV Global, which I have just acquired. You work for me."

"So? Are you unable to be professional because we had a brief interaction in the past?"

"Interaction," he scoffed. In *the past*? It was two short weeks ago. Still a very vivid memory that he relived at least once a day. In the shower. It was all he could do not to think of other uses for that counter ledge right now.

Dios, her effect on him was as strong as it had been when he'd first glimpsed her. Stronger, now that he knew what a volatile match they were. Distracting.

"What do you want to call it?" She held her chin up, mouth tight, stare as cold as ice. "You made it clear it was nothing significant. I feel the same."

Liar. She was too angry for him to believe that. And, try as he had to diminish it into a pleasant but trivial memory, he couldn't.

"Blame fate. She's having a laugh, I suppose." Her lips stretched in a facetious smile before she added in a mutter, "But if you think I made a *choice* to see you again, you're wrong."

He narrowed his eyes, surprised how deeply that got under his skin.

His phone pinged, notifying him of Oladele's email.

"She's on her way back." He unlocked the door and peeked out, then held it open. "My office."

CHAPTER FOUR

"You don't really intend to fire me," Siobhan said as she entered a room that was full of heavy furniture and the embedded funk of cigarette smoke. "You can't."

"I absolutely can," he contradicted. "I don't even need a reason beyond the fact I'm restructuring."

"But that's not fair. No one needs to know anything happened between us." How could he be so casually ruthless? Standing there with all the mesmerizing confidence that had attracted her so inexorably in the first place while only giving her half his attention as he read his phone?

"Six languages? You were taking your degree in that, weren't you?" he recalled. "Why Arabic?" He lifted his gaze from his phone, scrambling her brain in a new way.

"What are you reading?" She hurried toward him, trying to see while feeling exposed.

"Is this security reference authentic?" He expanded the PDF. "I supply components to TecSec. I know the man who signed this. *Personally.*"

"So do I. Obviously." She was standing too close. She was acutely aware of his height and the faint scent of his aftershave. That particular fragrance had been all over her skin that night until she had skulked back to her room and furiously scrubbed it off in the shower.

"How?" he demanded.

"Pardon? Oh." How did she know the man who ran one of the most elite security companies in the world? "That's confidential." She looked to her nails.

"I'll check it," he warned.

"Go ahead. Call him right now." She held his stare, but it wasn't easy when she knew that delving into her security clearance risked dredging up her connections. Her past.

The sting of that old humiliation began to scorch her cheeks.

He noticed.

For a few seconds, they were locked in a long stare. The atmosphere shifted from animosity to something else. Awareness. Sensual memories. *Pull.*

There was a tap on the door and Oladele entered.

They both took a quick step back from each other.

Oladele faltered, clearly sensing the crackle of tension. "Should I come back?"

"No. Come in." Joaquin flashed Siobhan a stern look that said *this isn't over*, but waved them to take a seat. "My team is on their way from Barcelona. Siobhan, advise the LV Global executive we're meeting in the board room in thirty minutes. I want to finalize this acquisition before my father finds yet another way to damage the ship."

Siobhan hadn't eaten since her avocado toast first thing this morning. It was closing on seven o'clock, but she had one more meeting to schedule before she left for the day. She was both limp with exhaustion and wired with adrenaline as she typed out the blessedly short agenda.

After Joaquin had unceremoniously ghosted her in San Francisco, she had done her best to turn the page. Thankfully, she'd been running flat out with the move and starting her new job. That meant that, until today, Joaquin had only intruded on her dreams, where he once again ran his hands and lips over her skin, setting her on fire with carnal need.

She always woke ashamed of herself, but now she was reeling at having seen him again. She was still reacting to the roller coaster of learning he was *not* married, but had definitely taken charge of her place of employment. Erotic spot fires shouldn't be cropping up at every turn, but they did, ambushing her with a flood of heated yearning followed by a cold bath of humiliation when she recalled the horrible way he'd left her.

Her heart kept stuttering with apprehension at the power he now had over her. It was bad enough he could axe her job with a word. Worse was the fact she was reacting to him as ferociously as she had that night. Her nerves were attuned to an awareness of him, ears pricked for the sound of his voice while a mortifying coal of sexual heat sat in the pit of her belly.

Work saved her to a point. It was a very busy day, but she stole one quick search of him online. It was another form of self-torture. She learned he'd been engaged at the time his brother had died eighteen months ago. The engagement had been broken off shortly after, but learning he'd been so close to another woman so recently made her feel…unsettled. He might not be married, but he'd been planning to marry. Knowing that added to the undercurrents between them as the day wore on.

After their altercation first thing this morning, she did everything she could to prove herself competent and reliable and professional. He only acknowledged her in a work capacity, which was to say, barely at all. She told herself that was a relief, but his brisk tone left a mark on her nerves. He'd spoken the same way to everyone, though. Things were very tense on all sides. She knew better than to take his attitude personally, but it felt like a fresh rebuff.

Not that she wanted his attention. Did she?

She didn't know what she wanted. She hadn't had a chance to process any of this, including the awe she'd felt as she watched him seize the leadership role. She had a lot of really strong men in her life and Joaquin could hold his own with any of them.

In a series of rapid-fire orders, he had delegated various tasks to her and Oladele, then brought them in to witness a battle royale in the meeting room. Joaquin had outlined to the LVG executives that the board had voted to allow his company, ProFab Worldwide, to assume LVG's debt. In exchange, he had gained controlling interest in the company. Lorenzo had been ousted. Joaquin was the king of the castle and restructuring began now.

Some department heads had sighed in relief. Others had been as outraged as Lorenzo.

Joaquin knew what he wanted, though. He had stated it clearly and didn't flinch under pushback. The first man who refused to carry out his instructions was dispassionately invited to leave and not come back. *Does anyone else wish to waste my time?*

Through it all, he hadn't acknowledged her with so much as a glance while she'd been riveted by him.

After a few more highly charged meetings, Joaquin had left for the day, but the building had continued to reverberate as the news traveled to all corners and his own team began meeting with the department heads. Siobhan and Oladele were some of the few people who got any work done. The rest were gossiping or responding to media requests. Others were frantically putting the word out that they were seeking alternate employment.

"It was a big day," Oladele said, stopping by her desk and startling her out of her reverie. "Expect the rest of the week to be the same."

"I've been thrown into the deep end before." Siobhan smiled weakly. "I don't mind."

"I can tell. You handle pressure very well." She cocked her head to give her a more penetrating look. "Including the concerns around your security clearance."

"They were understandable, given all that's going on. I didn't take offense."

That wasn't what Oladele was asking. She knew darned well more than a security check had prompted Joaquin's interest in her new EA. Siobhan wasn't about to admit she'd slept with their new boss, though.

"I have a million questions," Siobhan said. "But I'm sure things will clarify as the merger completes."

That's the language you will use, Oladele had told her this morning, even as Joaquin had been swinging in here like a pirate with a cutlass clenched in his teeth, taking the ship by force.

"Don't stay too late," Oladele warned.

"I'm leaving right after I send this. I'll see you in the morning."

Ten minutes later, Siobhan hit Send and got a text from an unknown number before she had finished belting her coat.

Are you still at the office? We need to talk.

Her pulse skipped. She knew exactly who it was, but replied, New phone, who dis?

Her phone rang immediately.

"Hola." She glanced around to ensure she was the only one in earshot. The floor was deserted, save for a janitor wiping down the break room. Even so, her nerves prickled as though she was doing something illicit yet titillating.

"I'm in my car." Joaquin's crisp voice abraded her nerves while fanning the heat in her middle. "I'm at least twenty minutes from the office. Traffic is a nightmare."

"That's why I take the metro." She forced a laissez-faire tone that was a complete fabrication.

"To where? Chamberí? That's where I was headed. I thought you would be home by now. I'll book you a car."

"You just said traffic is a nightmare."

"It is." He hissed out a curse. "I'll find a restaurant and text you the address."

"Why? No." There was a part of her that was…flattered? *Don't be stupid*, she quickly scolded herself. He didn't want to see her for romantic reasons. Today's acquisition had been very hostile. From what she'd gathered, Lorenzo had disowned Joaquin years ago. Joaquin probably still had doubts about her loyalty. "We've agreed nothing happened." It felt like a small victory to throw that in his face. "There's nothing else to say."

"We talk tonight or we don't talk at all," he said unequivocally.

He did want to fire her!

She looked at her phone, very tempted to tell him where he could shove this job and his arrogance, but she answered him anyway, "Oladele needs me, you know. This has been a very long day. I'm still in my work clothes. I want to go home, eat some instant noodles, then fall into bed. I'll see you tomorrow." So there.

"You're not eating instant noodles. I'll pick up takeout." He already ended the call.

What an annoying, domineering man. How had she ever found him attractive?

She knew how. *I'm interested. There's no improving on perfection.*

He had charmed her and she'd fallen for it. Duped again.

She shouldered her bag and left, wondering why he wanted to see her when it sounded as though he only wanted to dismiss her. He could do that with a memo from HR.

Losing her job was a distressing thought, but she didn't *need* to work the way some did. She had many fallback positions. She liked this job, though. She liked that she was supporting herself, building a relatively ordinary life where she was taken at face value, not seen as riding on nepotism or as a conduit to people who were more wealthy and powerful than she was.

What if he did want to see her for more personal reasons, though? The wicked, misguided trollop inside her gave a slither of glee, but she pushed her firmly back into her mental bedroom.

No. Nothing like that could happen between them. He might not be married, but he was her boss. And he'd walked out on her without a word in San Francisco, leaving her feeling discarded and devalued. She'd spent every day since trying to work out whether she was an idiot who didn't recognize a player when she met one, or trying to work out what she'd done in those last seconds that had been so horribly wrong he had run away the second she was out the door.

Her scorn carried her the rest of the way home, through the sea of commuters and holiday music.

She was genuinely exhausted as she walked from the station to her building, barely taking note of the festive bower of street decorations and the bustle of Christmas shoppers.

Her weariness made sense. She'd been pushing herself for a long time. She had tutored to support herself in Australia, refusing to live off the nest egg she'd accumulated in her previous life. The day after exams, she flew to London to see her mother. That had been her first stop before she visited her sisters in America while prepping and interviewing for six very different jobs, including two in California.

By the time she returned to Sydney, she had circumnavigated the globe inside of two weeks and hadn't adjusted to the time zone before she'd been on a plane for her new life here in Madrid. She'd started work the day after landing and still hadn't finished unpacking.

Maybe she would skip eating and go straight to bed, she decided as she approached the front of her building. More than anything, she needed to catch up on her sleep.

A car arrived at the curb beside her. Joaquin smoothly exited the backseat. He'd changed from his suit into a more casual pair of dark trousers with a pullover and a raincoat that hung open as he slammed the car door.

The charge of masculine energy that came off him was so electric, she felt it like a snap of static grounding through her. She disguised it by nodding at the insulated takeout bag he held.

"Side hustle?"

"Considering what I paid to clear my father's debts, I need one." He nodded at the front door. "Let's eat. I'm starving."

CHAPTER FIVE

She was famished, too, which left little fight in her. Siobhan brought him into the building, vibrating with awareness of him and nearly wilting with hunger when the food aromas filled the elevator.

Inside her flat, he glanced around as he removed his coat and accepted the hanger she offered before she removed her own coat.

It was an older building. The rooms were small, but bright. Both the living room and bedroom had a thin balcony that looked onto an alley and an even more ornate and visually pleasing building across the way. The wall between the bedroom and living room had been partially removed and fitted with a pair of frosted glass doors that she left open to create a more spacious feel.

She was a tidy person. The bed was made and there was only a discarded scarf on it that she had decided not to wear at the last minute this morning. It still felt...intimate, heightening her jumpiness at having him in her personal space.

He doesn't want you, she reminded herself. She didn't know why he was here, but it wasn't that.

She took the food into the kitchen. It was a narrow

galley that ended with a door into the minuscule bathroom, but the setup was efficient and it had a good-size pantry along with newish appliances.

Conscious of the impression he was gaining, she clarified, "It came furnished."

The sofa and chair were upholstered in a floral pattern that was too busy for her taste. She preferred contemporary styles and solid colors.

"I was lucky to find a sublet that I could get into right away. I love the location."

She never hung pictures of family so she would warm the space with paintings she'd purchased while living in Australia. They were on the floor, propped against the wall with framed, free-expression artwork made by her nieces and nephew.

She washed her hands, then set the table with the fragrant fideuà, which was a paella made with vermicelli noodles. It was piping hot and ready to serve in enameled cast-iron dishes with lids. Warm flatbread accompanied it along with tapenade, a salad and custard-filled buñuelos for dessert.

"Corkscrew?" he asked, showing her a bottle of white wine.

She handed it over with one glass. "None for me. If I have anything stronger than a glass of water, I'll be flat on the floor."

He set aside the bottle without opening it. "How hard has Oladele been working you?"

"It's not that." She refused to let him think she was anything but delighted by her job. "I haven't taken a proper break since before exams. Oladele said the office will close for Christmas on the nineteenth, though." That was only a week and a half away. "I'll catch up on my sleep then."

Oh, heck. She still had to finish her shopping for the children. Whether she joined her sister or not, she needed gifts for everyone.

"That's not the face of someone anticipating a break from work," he said, making her realize she'd revealed how daunted she was. And that he was watching her as closely as he had that night in San Francisco.

Disturbed, she explained, "I just remembered the Christmas shopping I have to finish."

"I wasn't sure if you celebrate. You don't have a tree." He flickered his gaze around her undecorated lounge.

"I haven't had time to get one." Truthfully, she hadn't made time. "My sister invited me to join them so there doesn't seem a point if I won't be here." That was her excuse for eschewing the wreaths and garlands she had once looked forward to hanging.

Last weekend, she had stayed with her nieces and nephew while Cinnia and Henri had flown to Paris for a function, hoping her weekend visit would excuse her from the holiday altogether, but the pressure had only increased.

You haven't had Christmas with us in five years, Cinnia had scolded. *Everyone wants you here. You know that.*

She did. And she wanted to see everyone. It wasn't the people she was avoiding. It was this time of year. She used to love all the joyful decor and festive traditions around Christmas, but these days they regressed her back to that heart-stopping moment when she'd realized how badly she'd messed up.

Pushing her dark thoughts aside, she waved an invitation for Joaquin to join her at the table. They both sat and tucked in without ceremony.

"You?" she asked, trying to make this extraordinary situation feel normal when all she could think about was the way they'd flirted over drinks and fallen on each other with a different type of hunger.

This was the meal he had promised to order for them before he had dumped her.

Why did she let that continue to sting? He'd made it clear they were ships passing even before they'd slept together, then told her afterward that he wasn't someone to plan to share things with.

She had slept with him knowing they weren't likely to have a future and she'd been fine with it. It was only in the afterglow, when she'd been anticipating going back to him for the rest of the night, that she had indulged a few expectations, wondering if maybe there *could* be more between them.

She lifted her gaze and found him watching her with a pull of dismay in his brows.

He was even more aloof and unreadable than he'd been in San Francisco.

Her stomach curdled anew with the fear she'd done something wrong. Offended or disappointed or repelled him in some way.

"I was only asking what you do at this time of year. If that's a state secret you don't care to share..." She was trying to be ironic, but the joke fell flat. She looked hopelessly at her food, appetite evaporating.

He let the silence hang for an extra second before stabbing his dish as though it needed killing before eating.

"My brother used to invite me to join him and Zurina. I always refused because our father was also invited. Last year, I gave in for the children's sake. It was their first Christmas without Fernando and it turned into hell because my father was there. We despise each other, as you may have gathered." He closed his lip over a mouthful, pensive as he chewed and swallowed.

She had gotten that memo. It had slapped her in the face this morning in the form of Lorenzo's rage.

"This year, Zurina and her parents are spending a few weeks in the Canary Islands," he continued. "I put them on my plane this afternoon. She asked me to join them, but I'll work. Prepping for today pushed my own projects to the back burner. I need to catch up."

"I'm still trying to understand what happened today," she admitted wryly.

"Same," he said with pithy sarcasm, flickering his gaze over her face and shoulders in a way that made her feel off balance.

She dropped her eyes, hating herself for *liking* the feel of his gaze. For quietly willing something more visceral out of him.

"I called Killian about your security clearance. He said he knows you through clients. He declined to tell me who they are, but said you were at liberty to reveal that information if you chose to."

"I don't." Her heart clenched in a pulse of discomfort.

Out in the street, there was a faint jangle of sleigh bells. It was the only noise for a few seconds, amplifying his silence.

"My partnership with Killian is reciprocal," Joaquin said. "I supply some of his hardware. He ensures my proprietary designs are well protected. He wouldn't set me up for industrial espionage when it could compromise his own interests, but I still find your presence in my father's company too convenient."

"For who?" she snorted.

"See? It's problematic for both of us."

"You can't fire me just because I accidentally had sex with you! I didn't know you were buying the company I was coming to work at." Dismissing her would be worse than mean-spirited. It was a betrayal of how vulnerable and uninhibited she'd been that night. He had already tossed her away like trash once for it.

"I can't afford mistakes right now."

"I didn't know I was one." She quit the table abruptly. Angrily. "I told you I hadn't slept with anyone in ages and this is why." She pointed at the floor between them. "I didn't want a man derailing me from my aspirations again." She had sensed that he had the power to pull her off course, but had found him enthralling enough to risk it. "I never dreamed you were the sort to deliberately sabotage my career. Out of misguided spite."

"I'll help you find something else—"

"Oh, don't do me any favors," she snapped. "I know people if I want to get hired through nepotism. I don't."

She paced across her small lounge, but when she reached the door to the balcony, she was compelled to yank the drapes to block out the colored lights on the neighbor's balcony. They were another throbbing reminder of that other time she had been profoundly stupid where a man was concerned.

Maybe if Joaquin understood that she really was okay with keeping a firm distance between them, he would let her stay? A pang of humiliation wrenched behind her navel. She refused to beg leniency from a man who had already made it clear he didn't want her.

She would fight for her job, though. He didn't get to take her dignity *and* her nascent career.

"I won't tell you who Killian's clients are, but I'll tell you why I went to Australia to start over," she decided, turning to face him. "I was living with some of them in London. The man I was seeing used me to get information on them." She still felt sick when she thought of it. Her eyes grew hot with remorse. With a ferocious desire to reverse time. To go back and not be so caught up in romantic ideals. She'd been so naive. So *oblivious*.

"Killian didn't do a background check?" He turned in his chair to face her more fully.

"Sometimes people aren't bad until they decide to be bad." She gritted her teeth at the nausea rising in her throat. "I'm not sure if he dated me in a long game or realized after we started seeing each other that being close to me could be profitable. Either way, he fooled me into believing we were in love." Self-contempt clenched in her chest.

His expression seemed to harden as the silence thickened, growing potent. Maybe that was her imagination, though. Why would he care about her feelings for another man beyond seeing her as foolish for falling for him?

"I like to think I'm smart." She forced herself to keep talking. "I already knew people could be self-interested, but he seemed different. Keen and…" He didn't need to hear all the ways she'd fallen for Gilbert's charms. "It was coming up to Christmas. He wanted to meet the people who were close to me." She brushed at a tickle on her cheek. "I brought him into a world where I was entrusted to help keep the jackals out."

Still, Joaquin didn't say anything while remorse sat like a jagged rock in her throat. It stayed heavy and thorny in her chest.

"He put together an exposé on them," she said shakily. "Not a bad light, but it revealed a lot of personal information. He thought he could do it anonymously. He tried selling the story with photos of their children, even though he knew the family worked hard to keep their faces out of the public eye." She started to tear up, *so* ashamed. So angry at Gilbert and herself.

"Did they manage to quash it?" he asked grimly.

"Yes. Thankfully, they have the money and influence to buy stories like that before they're published. Then some of Killian's professionals paid him a visit to ensure he didn't have copies. He was a promising engineer, but as far as I know he now runs a fish-and-chip truck in a dodgy part of London. The whole thing sits in my gut like an ulcer."

She gripped her elbows, still stinging with the humiliation at allowing herself to be used. At knowing he hadn't wanted *her*.

"I realize that doesn't make me seem like a reliable person to have on your payroll, but the fact is, I know what it's like to be manipulated by sex and emotion. I would never do that to anyone. It's horrible."

His cheek ticked once before he swore and looked away, then scrubbed his hand over his face.

"It's not just you." He rose and took a few agitated steps. "It's *him*."

"Who?" Her pulse skipped at the way he was suddenly in motion. "Your father?"

"Yes. He's the reason I left San Francisco without speaking to you." The look he flashed her held something that relit the spark in her chest that she was trying very hard to smother.

She clenched a fist against the sensation. *Don't fall for it*.

"What happened?"

He pinched the bridge of his nose, sighing heavily before he dropped his hand to reveal a weary expression, one that sent a ring of empathy through her.

"The minute you left that night, I picked up a message from Zurina. My father was trying to force her to marry him. She was very upset."

The woman in the scarf? "She's far too young for him."

"He's seventy-two. She's twenty-eight," he agreed grimly. "She's also a very wealthy woman. She brought her own fortune to the marriage and inherited Fernando's shares in LV Global along with his very lucrative investment portfolio and other properties, including the family vineyard that Lorenzo gifted them on their wedding day."

"He needs the money?"

"Yes," he said bluntly. "I didn't know how deeply in debt he is because I don't care to know. When Fernando passed, he seized the chance to return to the helm and I didn't fight him because LVG isn't something I wanted. But he immediately used its cash reserves to pay down debts to cronies. He's been taking on more debt ever since, putting the company at risk. Market forces have played a part, but Lorenzo's incompetence is the bigger issue. Fernando spent a decade moving the organization into the modern age. Lorenzo wants to take it back to what was familiar to him. He brought in his yes-men. They're all dinosaurs. You met some of them today." He waved a disparaging hand.

Does anyone else care to waste my time?

"He's been pushing aggressively toward what was tried and true thirty years ago. The board has been watching the place capsize in real time and were pressuring him to bring me aboard. He was teasing me with it, but he had no intention of giving it to me so we were at an impasse. If not for Zurina and the children, I would have let him drown in his own red ink. But I can't do that."

She could feel the frustration and animosity coming off him in dangerous, radioactive waves. It wasn't directed at her, but it was still intimidating.

"So you bought up the debt to oust him."

"Yes. Zurina's support was vital to my takeover today. Also, now that I have control of her interest in LVG, she has less value to my father. He should leave her alone, but we'll see." He pushed his hand through his hair.

"Doesn't that put you in his line of fire instead?" she asked with concern.

He shrugged that off, expression remaining hard. "I long ago accepted that he will plague me until one of us dies. I expect him to use any means to sabotage me, my company and LVG, now that I've stolen it from him." His gaze swung to her, landing with a crash. "That includes you."

"Me?" A clunking sensation swept through her limbs. "How could he use me? *Why* would he?"

"Because he exploits anything he perceives as a weakness." His graveled tone made her heart roll to a halt in her chest. "If he learns we're personally involved, he'll use it."

"But...we aren't," she said faintly, realizing they *couldn't* be.

She had thought he was treating her with such coldness because he didn't like her. Because he had regrets about San Francisco. She'd been feeling very brushed off and hurt.

Now her brain was catching up to the fact he'd left her for a family emergency. One with higher stakes than she could have imagined. He hadn't owed any explanations to a woman he'd spent an hour with, no matter how intimately they'd spent that time. He had believed he would never see her again. That was why he hadn't come to her door to tell her all of this then.

As her shell of umbrage cracked and fell away, so did most of her defenses against him. A need to help rose like a force inside her.

"Keep me on," she urged. "I will be a valuable asset

and no one will ever know we…" She swallowed whatever words might have described the way they'd knotted themselves together, wringing so much pleasure from a brief hour. "I promise."

She wasn't pleading for her job as much as a chance to keep seeing him, if only from afar.

His mouth tightened. The way he delved into her eyes with his narrowed gaze made her feel obvious. Naked. As though he read her motives as clearly as a neon sign.

His cheek ticked. Did he feel it, too? The temptation? The *want*?

A hot pressure of desperation arrived behind her breastbone. She looked away, blinking, trying to douse it with a measured breath.

"Fire me, then. I don't care," she lied while anguish slithered in her belly.

"You can stay," he said abruptly. "For now." He moved to the closet. "We won't talk of this again. San Francisco didn't happen."

She nodded jerkily while a flip-flopping sensation of relief and disappointment nearly pushed a whimper from her throat. This was what she wanted, wasn't it? She would keep her job. He wouldn't interfere in her life.

A weight sat on her chest as she came to the door and watched him shrug on his overcoat, though. A sense of lost potential. Deep in her fanciful brain, she had thought maybe destiny had brought them together again.

The reality was they hadn't had any sort of connection beyond sexual. She'd been a release valve for him at a time he was under a lot of pressure. Now that was firmly in the past.

"There's something I wished I'd done before you left my room that night," he said with a hard set to his jaw.

"What's that?" she asked, lifting her gaze with surprise.

"I should have said goodbye properly." His hand arrived at her waist and the other cradled the side of her neck, dragging her close.

Time turned to gelatin, making each movement slow and deliberate and profound. Her hands slid upward of their own accord, arriving at his shoulders to twine around his neck. She rose on tiptoe, offering her mouth without speaking another word, and dove her hand into the hair at the back of his head, urging him down.

Because she had longed for this, too. She had needed to know if it had been as good as she imagined.

It was.

As his lips sealed over hers, a sob left her, one of pain because the electric sensation of kissing him was too intense. It rang like a bell through her arms and across her chest, urging her grip to tighten around his neck. To cling. Because they couldn't *do* this.

For a long minute they did, though. They held fast to each other while they said *hello* and *I remember* and *goodbye* in the same long, poignant kiss. The thickness of his erection nudged against her aching mound and he could have easily taken her to her bed. She was ready to drag him there herself.

But he drew back abruptly, as though being wrenched from her by an invisible force.

It stung like a tear. Her heart pounded loud enough to deafen her ears. She kept her eyes closed, not wanting to face the inevitable. Not wanting him to see how utterly he owned her when he was, once again, the one pulling away.

She heard him take one shaken breath and the door closed behind him.

"See you tomorrow," she whispered.

CHAPTER SIX

JOAQUIN COULDN'T AFFORD a single misstep. Lorenzo had retreated to his town house after the board overthrew him, but he was back at the office in the morning with a phalanx of lawyers, trying to retake his mantle.

Joaquin was no longer the teenaged boy with a black eye and nothing in his pockets, though. He had his own resources. He met his father inside the revolving door to the street with his own lawyers, a half dozen security guards and a "go quietly and this is yours" settlement offer.

After taking the envelope from Oladele, he held it out.

Lorenzo knocked it from his hand, berating him loudly for all the staff to hear as they hurried in from the street and headed to the elevator.

"You're making a fool of yourself." Joaquin cut through his tirade. "Take that offer. It includes a profit share in the estate in La Rioja and expires at midnight."

His father's hair nearly came off his head. "You can't take that from me! I gave it to your brother. It comes back to me."

"It will be secured in trust for your grandchildren." The sprawling vineyard was highly profitable and was another reason Lorenzo had pressured Zurina to marry him. "If you want a benefit from it, take that offer." Joaquin nodded at the floor, refusing to pick up the envelope.

"You think you're getting the better of me, don't you?" Lorenzo stepped forward to poke his chest.

"I've never seen anything but the worst of you." Joaquin curled his lip. "Touch me again and you'll see the worst of *me*."

As he stared down his father, his inner antennae prickled. Siobhan walked by in his periphery.

Joaquin didn't look, but he caught tall boots kicking a tweed skirt as she circled their group. Their kiss last night had tasted like champagne and hunger. Like the things they'd done when they had wrecked a hotel bed. Like the things he wanted to do with her again.

Leaving her last night had nearly pulled his soul from his body. He'd definitely left a piece of himself there with her.

But even though he felt her gaze on him, he didn't *allow* himself to look at her. It would betray his interest to Lorenzo.

Lorenzo looked at her, though. Among his thousands of faults, he was a lecher for young women, which was objectionable any day of the week. Today his attention on Siobhan was beyond galling. It was revolting.

"Leave now," Joaquin said in gritty warning.

Lorenzo swung his gaze back to Joaquin's, teeth bared in a sneer. He was trying to work out whether Joaquin's hostility was purely due to his presence here or if it had gone up a notch upon Siobhan's arrival.

Oladele picked up the envelope and handed it to one of Lorenzo's lawyers.

"This isn't a negotiation. It's that or nothing." Joaquin pointed at the envelope.

His father spit on Joaquin's shoes.

Joaquin spit right back and held his father's glare of outrage. He would not back down. Not anymore.

Siobhan stood transfixed as she watched Oladele set a hand on Joaquin's sleeve in a gentle signal to hold his temper in check.

"This isn't over," Lorenzo declared before storming out.

The elevator pinged next to her. Siobhan scrambled to grasp at the door, waiting while Joaquin strode toward her with his entourage of suits.

She had taken far too long deciding what to wear today, eventually choosing a short jacket in earthy brown over a tweed skirt with a fedora to protect her hair from the rain. She offered a hesitant smile as Joaquin approached, but his gaze skimmed past her, making her stomach clench in embarrassment at trying to engage him.

She looked to the floor, still confused by his kiss after making it so clear to her that they couldn't be anything but boss and employee.

Everyone stepped into the elevator. No one spoke as it rose, but the air was thick with undercurrents. She picked out Joaquin's aftershave among the other fragrances in the small space and drew it deep, filling her nostrils with the tangy, tangible feel of his cheek brushing her jaw. His hungry lips devouring hers.

Her face felt stiff with the effort of maintaining a neutral expression. It took all her effort not to glance at him as she departed with Oladele onto their floor.

She tried very hard not to betray her awareness of Joaquin, but within hours, they were called to the boardroom next to his office.

Others were already there, including Joaquin's assistant, a young man she'd met briefly yesterday. Siobhan sent him a friendly, "Good morning."

The other man returned her smile with a warm one of his own that quickly turned to a daunted look aimed beyond her shoulder.

She followed his line of sight to Joaquin.

He hit her with a cool stare of disapproval, one that peeled a layer from her composure, leaving her raw.

With an indignant lift of her chin, she took her seat behind Oladele while Joaquin shifted his attention to his laptop.

"Lorenzo has rejected the settlement offer and has begun a counterassault. He is claiming to still be CEO until the shareholders vote otherwise. He's also smearing my reputation and bringing ProFab into it." That was Joaquin's company in Barcelona. "Pursue defamation charges. He must have signed nondisclosure agreements that prevent him from discussing the inner workings of LVG. See if he's still bound by that."

Oladele nodded and glanced at Siobhan to make a note.

"I'll look into the D&O liability insurance, too,"

Siobhan said. "Directors and officers," she explained as everyone looked at her. "Its purpose is to cover unintentional negligence, but if he was the CEO, and deliberately causes the devaluation of his company, he could be exposing himself to legal consequences. There may be a means to pursue charges. Perhaps letting him know that would encourage him to back down."

Oladele made an approving noise and several heads nodded, but Joaquin only pinned her with an inscrutable look before turning his attention to the head of accounting, requesting an audit to prove that his father had been fabricating numbers during his tenure.

The meeting broke up and Joaquin walked out, leaving a wake of relieved exhales behind him.

As everyone rose, Oladele said, "Siobhan, will you ask Joaquin if he's had a chance to review the documents I sent this morning? I have to return this call."

"Of course." Overcoming a wave of trepidation, Siobhan went to his door, which was open. He was standing at his desk, tapping on the keyboard of his laptop. She knocked.

"Come in. Close the door," he said as he saw her.

"Oh. I'm only here to ask…" She slipped in and pressed the door closed behind her. "Oladele is wondering if you've had time to review the documents she sent?"

"I was about to do it. What's going on with you and my assistant? HR frowns on office romance."

She stood taller, insulted when his assistant was a virtual stranger and *San Francisco didn't happen.*

"Has the policy changed?" she asked archly. "Because

I read all of them when I onboarded. HR asks to be informed of romantic relationships to mitigate liability. If necessary, they will transfer employees without penalty." She responded to his elevated brow with a sugary smile. "I do my homework."

"Is that the long way of saying *nothing*?"

"Yes." The heat of humiliation began climbing from her throat. "I know you think I'm fast, but I'm not frequent about it." She turned to yank on the door latch so she didn't have to stand here boiling in his ugly judgment of her.

"I didn't say that," he growled behind her.

"You implied it." She pulled on the door.

"Wait," he commanded.

She set her teeth and held the door open, forcing a bored expression onto her face as she turned back to him.

"That was a good idea about the D&O insurance," he said begrudgingly. "It won't work—"

"Is that a compliment? Because you've buried it," she mocked.

"Lorenzo doesn't scare easily," he continued without reacting to her sarcasm. "But I can see that you're looking for fresh angles of attack. That's the sort of ingenuity I appreciate in the people who work for me. Let me know if you find something with teeth."

Oh. He really was complimenting her.

Was she supposed to say thank you? You're welcome?

She definitely wasn't supposed to stand here gawking while he said impassively, "Anything else?"

"No." She left, flushed and disconcerted by the entire exchange.

* * *

The rest of the week passed in similar encounters where Joaquin largely ignored her unless she had the nerve to speak up. He never berated her for offering an opinion, but he didn't express overt appreciation again.

She kept reminding herself that they had both agreed—that she wanted as much as he did—to leave their one-night stand in the past.

But she still experienced a thrill of anticipation each time Oladele said, "We're needed upstairs."

Simply being in a room with Joaquin wired her with excitement.

"I know this has been a demanding time," Joaquin said on Friday afternoon, wrapping up a meeting in the boardroom where someone had brought homemade polvorónes, a shortbread-style cookie, and anise-flavored crumble cookies called mantecados. "You've earned your weekend. Rest up and give me your best for one more week. Then we can all relax through the Christmas break."

Rather than leave as he usually did, he hung back to answer a question from someone in PR.

"Gracias," Siobhan murmured as she moved past them.

"Oh, that's you, Ms. Upton," Joaquin said with an ironic quirk of his mouth. "I didn't recognize you in your glasses."

Her pulse tripped over the fact he had noticed her at all, let alone such a tiny detail. She touched the navy-blue frames.

"Is that a joke?" She couldn't believe he was making one, not that he had failed to recognize her.

"Yes." The corner of his mouth indented with self-deprecating amusement.

Someone said something about superhero disguises and conversation turned to the latest blockbuster scheduled to release over the holidays.

She followed the crowd to the elevators, not letting herself look back, but she was still replaying his remark, shyly gratified to have provoked his almost-smile.

"Siobhan." Oladele hurried out from her office as Siobhan arrived at her desk. "This was delivered by courier while we were upstairs." She handed over an envelope. "Joaquin needs to see it. See if you can catch him before he leaves."

Siobhan hurried back to the elevator, past his assistant at the reception desk, and found him locking his office door at the end of the empty corridor.

"Oh, good. I thought I might miss you." She strode toward him. "Oladele said this was left on her desk while we were in the meeting." She halted as she reached him, but had the strangest sensation of continuing forward. She slapped a hand on the wall, catching her balance, alarmed.

A firm hand wrapped around her arm. "Are you all right?"

"No," she said reflexively. "Yes. I'm not sure. Just a little dizzy. I think I caught a bug."

Heat suffused her at the way his grip eased, but his hand stayed on her arm. She looked at it, wondering if he could feel the way her muscles were melting and her blood was turning to honey.

He released her and his fingers rubbed into his palm.

She adjusted her glasses and cleared her throat. "I was with my sister's kids last weekend. I love them to death, but children are walking petri dishes."

"Reason number one million why I never plan to have them." He shook the pages from the opened envelope.

"Really? That surprises me."

He paused to lift his gaze, snagging hers without effort.

She didn't know how to interpret that and quickly babbled, "It's just that I read you were engaged last year. That suggests you were planning to start a family."

"Siobhan. This conversation is inappropriate." He used an even tone and he wasn't wrong, but she took his remark like a slap. One she deserved.

He had expressed a normal concern for a coworker and she had let it devolve into telling him her life history and admitted to looking him up. Bringing up his romantic history, asking him about his plans to have children, was totally offside. The fact that *they* had a history between them pushed her inquiry from nosy into the sort of thing one asked an intimate partner as a compatibility check.

While her cheeks flamed with chagrin, she glanced over her shoulder. The doors to the corridor were closed, but they might not be as alone as they thought. His assistant had still been at his desk by the elevators. There could be stragglers in the boardroom.

"I'm sorry," she said, stricken and unable to raise her eyes to see what was in his expression. "I'll go." She pivoted one foot.

"Let me see what this is first," he muttered and glanced over the cover letter then swore tiredly. "My father is taking LV Global to court. This is what sort of man he is." He fluttered the pages in impotent fury. "He would rather lock me into years of court appearances and legal fees, demonstrating to the entire world that he is no longer fit to run this company, than accept that irrefutable fact. Give this back to Oladele. Tell her we'll discuss it Monday. Then go home and get some rest."

She wordlessly took the papers, fighting to keep her chin up as he walked alongside her to the elevator. Did he *have* to step into it with her? The space felt so claustrophobic she could hardly breathe. She kept replaying her *inappropriate* words, feeling unbearably gauche.

"You could make this easier," he said as the elevator descended. "Wear ugly clothes. Stop showering."

They were both staring straight ahead. For a second, she wondered if she had heard him correctly. Then she thought about telling him *that* was inappropriate, but a tiny glow flickered to life in her chest and began to expand, warming her to her fingertips and toes.

Every day she came to work anticipating her moments with him, and every day she felt tortured by them. Let down, even. She thought about their kisses and their lovemaking far too often. She reminded herself constantly that they weren't going back to that.

But he seemed to be telling her that he still felt this awareness, too. This attraction.

As the elevator stopped on her floor, she said, "I'm probably carrying a deadly plague."

The doors opened.

"See? Was that hard?" he drawled.

She bit back her pleased smile as she walked away.

CHAPTER SEVEN

SIOBHAN IGNORED JOAQUIN'S order to rest and spent the weekend Christmas shopping.

She even made a point of watching children who were blinking in wonderment at toys and pausing to listen to a choral group singing before a massive decorated tree, trying to remind herself why she used to love Christmas so much.

It cheered her a little, but she couldn't seem to shake a leaden feeling in her limbs. No actual sniffles or cough arrived, though. She wasn't running a fever or even feeling achy. She was merely tired and her stomach was a little unsettled so she stuck to bland foods and skipped coffee and wine, hoping to feel better by Monday.

She didn't, but she wasn't any worse so she didn't feel justified calling in sick. There was still so much to do and she didn't want to let Joaquin down.

She didn't want to miss a chance to see him. That was the real reason.

You could make this easier.

She'd been deeply stung when he had rebuffed her remark about his engagement. All she had been able to learn online was that it had been announced a few weeks before his brother passed and was called off shortly after. But he was right. It was very personal and none of her business. She shouldn't have brought it up at work or anywhere else.

She had been deeply surprised by his *reason one million* for not wanting children, though. It had struck a pang of distress in her because she wanted children someday. She didn't really believe in fate, either, but the way she and Joaquin had come together so coincidentally after parting in San Francisco had made her secretly wonder if greater forces were conspiring to throw them together.

His aversion to children told her they weren't as sympatico as she'd hoped. Not that she should have any hopes where he was concerned. Even if he was physically attracted to her, his remark in the elevator told her he didn't want to be.

She wished she had his Teflon air of aloofness. It was taking all her effort to hide her crush on her boss while he looked through her half the time and, when he did acknowledge her, put up barriers so quickly afterward, it was like walking into a glass wall, halting her in her tracks.

Despite that, she inwardly jumped for joy when she picked up an email from him, addressed to her and Oladele.

I'll be meeting with investors all week. I don't want any delay in responding to my father's legal action. My assistant has instructions that I can be interrupted at any time if you need my signature or authorization to keep things moving.

Twice that day, Oladele handed Siobhan a folder and asked her to run upstairs. Twice Siobhan gave strangers an apologetic smile while she patiently waited for Joaquin to skim the paperwork and sign off.

"I'm confused," she told Oladele when she returned the second time. "Why is he meeting investors individually? It doesn't seem very efficient. Why doesn't he hold a conference call and be done with it?"

"My educated guess is that these are his own investors in ProFab. Lorenzo is trying to undermine him, suggesting Joaquin took on too much debt by purchasing LVG. Lorenzo wants them to pressure Joaquin to back off, but he's reassuring them instead, and doing it in Lorenzo's office, which is a nice touch." Oladele's mouth quirked.

Siobhan had to admire the power move. "I guess coming here shows them what he's purchased, too."

"The personal touch will have a ripple effect. Word will spread," Oladele added.

It was the sort of tactic Siobhan's brother-in-law would use. Why host a press conference if a whisper campaign was more effective?

She started back to her desk, then paused.

"Can I ask… How did you meet Joaquin?" That wasn't really what she wanted to know.

"Through Fernando. Joaquin sometimes came to the parties he and Zurina hosted." Oladele gave her a circumspect look. "If you're asking if I conspired with Joaquin to oust Lorenzo, I did not. I could tell the board was leaning toward handing things to Joaquin, but Zurina spearheaded that. Lorenzo left me a voice mail the morning it happened, asking why the board was meeting without him. I didn't know it was happening until it was."

"I'm sorry. I wasn't implying that you acted improperly. I know you wouldn't," Siobhan assured her.

"I don't think you would act improperly, either." Oladele held her gaze for an extra millisecond, allowing the significance of her statement to sink in before she switched back to work mode. "Can you get Señora Perez on the phone for me?"

"Of course."

Oladele knew, *knew* there was more to Siobhan's relationship with Joaquin than either of them admitted to. Should she confess that their romance had lived and died before she got here?

Tuesday was more of the same. As Siobhan was searching through old records, Oladele handed her a folder.

"Upstairs?" Siobhan guessed.

"Sí, por favor."

Siobhan hurried to the elevator with too much eagerness. She waved the folder at Joaquin's assistant, who nodded at her to approach the inner sanctum. She moved down the hall, past the empty boardroom and paused when she found a bodyguard stationed at Joaquin's door.

It was the first time she'd seen one here, but it was a fairly normal sight to her because Cinnia and all of her in-laws employed them. That was how Siobhan knew Killian. He handled all the security for her sister's family. Siobhan had taken self-defense classes with one of his instructors when she'd been a teenager and still practiced on a regular basis.

She showed her work badge to the man, but before she could knock, the door was pulled inward.

Joaquin's voice was saying, "—appreciate your making time—"

He cut himself off as he noticed her.

"¿Firma, por favor?" She waved the folder as an explanation and stepped back to allow his guest to exit. Her cheeks warmed with pleasure at how arrested Joaquin had seemed by the sight of her, though.

"Give my best to your family," Joaquin said absently.

"I will," promised a male voice as a strange man stepped out.

Siobhan had conjured a polite smile for Joaquin's guest, but it fell off her face. He wasn't a stranger at all. The handsome man in his forties was very well-known to her.

"Dorry," he said with surprise.

"Ramon." Siobhan breathed the name with shock and enough familiarity to raise Joaquin's hackles.

He'd started to open the door and found her unexpectedly outside it. In that millisecond of being hit by the sight of her, he'd been taken aback by how beautiful she was. By how *pleased* he was to see her.

Today she wore a thick gray knit dress that fell to the tops of her knee-high boots. A chunky belt of square silver links nipped at her waist, and its neckline draped like a scarf. Nothing about it was particularly sexy or daring, but she made it look runway chic.

Then Ramon Sauveterre stepped out and *hugged* her.

A deeply regressive emotion exploded through Joaquin. He clamped down on it, but the atavistic taste for blood stayed on his tongue.

Because Siobhan hugged Ramon back. And she offered the other man a bemused, untampered laugh. Not the kind she muted as quickly as it formed, the way she'd been doing around here, if she suddenly realized he was watching her. This was natural and lovely and full of genuine affection.

"It's good to see you." Ramon hung on to her arms, continuing to smile fondly at her. "I knew you'd taken a job in Madrid. I didn't know it was here. I've already sent the family south, but I wanted to take this meeting." He glanced at Joaquin with bemusement.

Whatever was in Joaquin's face erased Ramon's good-natured humor. He pulled his brows together. The temperature in the corridor dropped several degrees.

"I do work here." Siobhan's tone grew reproachful. "And everyone here knows me as Siobhan."

"Oh, hell." Ramon gave his jaw a rub then held out his palm. "My bad, but when have I ever had to call you that?"

"Today. Right now. This is the moment you were supposed to call me that."

They shared a look of laughter and apology and history. So much history it made Joaquin want to pull Siobhan into his office and lock out everyone else, most especially his too-suave business partner.

Joaquin had never been a jealous person. He hadn't been allowed to be. He'd had a taste of it with his assistant last week and learned the emotion didn't sit well with him. At all.

"*How* are you two acquainted?" he asked coolly.

"Oh. Um." Siobhan folded her arms and flickered a look between them.

"I'll let you fill him in." Ramon gave her shoulder a squeeze. "My plane is waiting. Do you need a lift? Should I wait for you?"

"No, I need to work, but thank you. I'll see you again soon."

Ramon kissed both her cheeks, needling the green monster within Joaquin before he gave Joaquin a last thoughtful look and left with his bodyguard.

Joaquin opened his door wider and jerked his head at Siobhan to enter.

"What—" he said as he pushed the door closed with a hard click "—was that?"

"Someone I know." She shrugged it off, avoiding his gaze as she set the folder on his desk. "Oladele is waiting for this. Do you mind? I have a lot of work that needs to be finished by end of day, and the big boss is looking for any excuse to fire me." She delivered the facetious remark with a distant smile that could have come from his own arsenal.

He hated it.

"Tell me." He approached the desk and closed his hand over the pen she held out, capturing her fingers in his grip. Not tightly. Just enough to hold her full attention. Just enough to hold *her* and convince himself she was, in some small way, his. For now.

"You're asking me to share something highly personal." She could have pulled her hand away, but she didn't. Her chin went up a notch. Her lashes flickered and he thought her breath stuttered. "Too personal for the workplace." *Inappropriate*, her defiant glare said as she slid a pointed glance to his grip on her hand.

She was getting back at him for that day in the corridor, when he'd told her she was out of line with her personal question about children. He'd felt small when he'd slapped it down, but every moment around her was a struggle. Even as he commuted to the office, before he saw her, he would wonder what she would be wearing today. Hair up or down? Glasses or contacts? Heels or boots? Did he have a meeting scheduled that would bring her up to his floor? Or did he have to engineer a glimpse of her from afar?

Then, when he did see her, he had to fight the urge to fall into bantering with her. He fought standing too close. Fought asking her to dinner. Fought pulling her near—

He wanted to yank her into his arms right now.

He let go of her hand.

The pen dropped to the desktop.

"Tell me how you know him or I'll imagine you were lovers." He drew the folder closer, pretending disinterest even though his vision was still violent green.

She made a choked noise. "Why would you care if we were?"

"I care," he ground out and jerked up his head.

Her breath cut in and her eyes flared wide at whatever she read in his face. Her mouth softened and her jaw went slack.

Angry with himself for revealing so much, frustrated at this sensation of being eaten alive, he said bitingly, "I thought you had hard boundaries around adultery. He's been married for years. They have children."

"I know that," she said with a flash of her own temper. "My sister is married to his brother."

"Henri?" Joaquin had met Ramon's identical twin on more than one occasion along with both their wives. "Your sister is Cinnia?" The resemblance seemed obvious now as he looked past Siobhan's dark hair. "This is the wealthy family you're related to?"

"Yes." She folded her arms and radiated defensiveness. "Why does it matter?"

Because *wealthy* was a gross understatement. Joaquin was wealthy. The Sauveterre family, two pairs of identical twins, were celebrities. The younger pair of girls was *royalty*. The family's wealth and fame had made them targets, though. When Ramon and Henri had been teenagers, one of their sisters had been kidnapped. She'd been recovered and all the siblings were married with children of their own now, but they still maintained a heavy security presence as a precaution.

"When your boyfriend took those unauthorized photos, it was them?"

"Ex," she corrected tightly. "Yes. Ramon's children. I was staying with them while I went to Cambridge."

"Why?"

"I was working on my language degree."

"Why were you staying with them?" he spelled out.

"Because I was going to Cambridge," she said with exasperation. "Ramon was working out of the London office. Izzy had just had their twins. They had nannies, but I had already helped Cinnia with their twins and Izzy doesn't have siblings. She didn't have a network in London and needed someone she…" She cleared her throat. "Someone she could trust. It seemed like a win-win for me to stay with them."

"But it wasn't? Because of what your ex did?"

"I don't want to talk about it." Her shoulders hunched in disgrace.

"Why did Ramon call you Dorry?" he asked in confusion.

"I told you I changed my name."

"Yes, but why?"

"Why do you want to know?" Her voice thinned with persecution.

"Because you don't need this job." He stabbed at his desktop. "Which makes me wonder why you fought so hard to keep it."

"Oh, my *gawd*," she muttered, striding toward the pair of sofas that faced each other over a coffee table. "You're right. I don't need to work. Henri has been paying me an outrageous allowance since I went to live with him and Cinnia at fourteen, when she had *their* twins."

"They didn't have nannies?"

"Yes, but Cin was actually very sick when she delivered them and they were taken by C-section. Plus, she and Henri had just got back together. He thought she would feel isolated if she didn't have family around. I was already homeschooling and helping Cin with her estate practice so it made sense. I stayed because I liked being part of their family." Her voice softened and she traced the seam on the back of the sofa. "Henri's siblings all treated me like I was one of them. It was nice."

"He still supports you?"

"No." She crinkled her brow at him. "You must know their family history, that Henri's sister was kidnapped when they were young?"

"Of course." It had dominated the headlines, especially here in Spain.

"Henri is very careful about security because of that. He wanted me to live with them because he knew I was safe there. He put me through the self-defense courses that Cin and his sisters took and I was drilled on all the security protocols. I knew what was at stake and didn't make social profiles, but Dorry Whitley was well-known enough that if people heard my name, they would ask me about them. I learned to spot when I was being befriended because someone wanted access to them. Then I missed one."

"What's his name?"

"Putrid McDogmeat." She stood with her arms folded, back stiff. "I had always felt wrong about accepting Henri's support. It felt as though I was being paid to be Auntie Dorry. When I put Ramon's children at risk…" She shuddered. "I couldn't be on the family payroll after that."

"Did Henri blame you? Because Ramon doesn't seem to be holding any grudges."

"No. They've always been very magnanimous. Ramon says it was his mistake because he allowed me to introduce Gilbert to his children. But it was *my* mistake. *I* dated the man. *I* vouched for him." She turned to stab between her breasts. "I couldn't stay with them after that. And I didn't want any footprints leading back to them, either. I moved to Australia and asked Killian to give me a new ID and school records, so I wasn't Dorry Whitley anymore. I kept a low profile, worked my butt off for top grades and got this job on my own merit. That actually means a lot to me. I *like* being Siobhan Upton."

Joaquin leaned his hip on the desk. "That's not the only reason, though, is it?"

"For what?"

"For changing your name. You don't want to be Dorry because you're mad at her. You're punishing her."

"No." She scowled into the middle distance, mouth twitching sullenly. "Maybe. I deserve to be punished. It was a horrible, dangerous mistake."

"You're being too hard on yourself."

"You're entitled to your opinion even if you're wrong." She looked to the side.

He snorted and moved close enough to catch her gaze. "I'm never wrong. Like you, I'm perfect. Never make mistakes."

She frowned, mouth pouting. "Can you please—" she cleared her throat "—not tell anyone who I am?"

"I won't say a word," he assured her.

"Thank you." Her shoulders relaxed. "I just don't want people to…"

"I understand." It was a lot to carry. He was annoyed that Henri had put that much pressure on her, but he also had the impression she put a lot on herself.

Dios, her scent went to his head when he stood this close. It wasn't bold enough to be perfume. It was a subtle combination of shampoo and hand cream and the summer peach fragrance of *her*. He searched for its source, gaze tracking into her throat then back to her cheeks.

She tilted her head back and her gaze tangled with his. She licked her lips.

He was a man, not a machine. With temptation this close and the nip of jealousy still in his blood, his resistance to her all but vanished. He hooked his finger in her belt and tugged, inviting her closer.

She flowed into him so he was able to slide his arms around the soft column of her. His mouth found hers and her taste washed through him. Lust flexed its claws deep into his skin, fueling his hands in their quest to map her shape and meld her to his front.

"Joaquin," she moaned as he sought the fragrant skin of her throat. Her arms climbed behind his neck so it was no effort at all to hitch her hips onto the back of the sofa and push her skirt up, exposing her thighs in thin black leggings to his restless hands.

This was where he had longed to be again. He pushed deeper into the V of her thighs until he felt the heat of her against the ridge of his erection. Until her mouth was firmly under his again so he could devour her.

The wrinkled suede of her boots pressed erotically against the backs of his legs, urging him to press harder. The gorgeous weight of her breast filled his hand, her nipple pebbled firmly enough he could feel it through the knit. He set his other hand on her tailbone, the bar of his arm keeping her from falling to the cushions while he ground himself against her.

She said something. It could have been a demand or a

plea. He didn't know. All he knew was that he was starving and needed this. *Her.*

As lust began to overwhelm him, compelling him to claim her, he drew her back onto her feet and turned her to face the back of the sofa.

She gasped and thrust her ass against his fly, crushing the ridge of his erection in the most delicious way. He dragged her skirt up and caught the waistband of her leggings, starting to drag them down, revealing her round ass and the midnight-blue lace that cut across her cheeks.

He followed the dark line of color with his fingertips into the crevice of her thighs, seeking the heat. The dampness. The welcoming clasp of her sheath as he delved into paradise.

She moaned in a way that stroked him like velvet and arched her back. Inviting him to explore deeper. To take.

Condom, he thought and glanced around, only then seeing where he was.

He cursed crudely and pulled his touch away too roughly, pulling back from her so abruptly, she gasped in shock and clung to the sofa while she sent him a wild look over her shoulder.

"What's wrong?"

She was nearly irresistible with that sensual flush and her heavy eyelids and her pupils shot wide with passion.

"I didn't lock the door. *This* is a dangerous mistake, Siobhan." She *worked* for him.

She gasped and yanked her clothes back into order, mouth taking on a bruised pout, eyes wide with speechless hurt. Her ankle wobbled and he tried to steady her, but she disdainfully pulled from his touch.

"Leave the folder with your assistant," she said in a hollow voice. "I need the ladies' room."

"Siobhan." He took a step to go after her, then stopped himself. *Damn it*.

He was her employer. He couldn't *do* this.

How had this even happened. He had been succeeding at treating her like any other employee until— No. He hadn't. If he was brutally honest with himself, he would recognize that even when he wasn't overstepping boundaries, he was a little harder on her, a little slower to offer praise, taking care not to reveal so much as a hint of favoritism toward her.

He was trying to *protect* her, though. She saw every day the lengths Lorenzo would go to strike at him. Surely, she understood why this couldn't happen?

Who could comprehend it, though? Really? He didn't fully understand Lorenzo's hatred of him. Lorenzo had been equally hard on Fernando, but had at least acknowledged Fernando's position as his heir and groomed him accordingly. For years it had merely been favoritism of one son over the other, but once Lorenzo had been back here at LVG, it had become outright efforts to sabotage Joaquin. Why?

Yes, he'd been a boisterous child, always getting into things. He saw the same energy and curiosity in his nephew and knew it was easy to see that behavior as defiance.

We caught him putting his dinosaurs in the toaster, Fernando had said of the boy during one of their last conversations. *Pulled a chair over to reach it. He wanted to know what would happen.*

Fernando had been nonplussed, but proud of the boy's ingenuity and desire to experiment.

Lorenzo had never been proud of Joaquin, though. He'd saved his praise for Fernando, who'd been smart and athletic, but also deferential and disciplined. Lorenzo had blamed his wife for Joaquin's strongmindedness. *Teach him his place*, Lorenzo had told her many times.

Then his mother had left and Lorenzo had taken on putting Joaquin in his place with his own firm hand. Fernando had intervened as often as he could, but Lorenzo had swung enough at both of them that it made little difference. He preferred to punish his youngest, though. The one who didn't matter.

There were times Joaquin had kept himself on a tight leash, thinking maybe, if he was good enough, his mother would come back. She had sworn to him that Lorenzo had driven her away, not him, but he still blamed himself. He was too quick to speak out, always determined to find a way to whatever he wanted even if he would be punished for it.

He knew now that his mother had taken the brunt of Lorenzo's anger until she feared for her life, never dreaming her husband would turn on their sons. Then Lorenzo had undermined her financially and socially, making it impossible for her to gain custody of them.

Eventually, Joaquin had realized how much abuse she had taken on his behalf and, in a twisted way, was glad she had left so he didn't have to worry about her.

Then there was Esperanza. Joaquin never would have engaged himself to her if he had known he would wind up back in his father's sphere. From the moment Lorenzo was introduced to her at Fernando's wake, Lorenzo had behaved intolerably toward her. When she broke their engagement a few weeks later, Joaquin knew it was for the best that she distance herself from him.

Women didn't fare well when they were attached to him. Even his brief liaisons were fraught with the same thing that was plaguing Siobhan right now—he was aloof. Inaccessible. Not outwardly cruel, but carrying a history that left him stunted. Unable to attach.

Women left him and he let them go for their sake and his own.

He wasn't letting Siobhan go, though. He kept trying to make himself relegate her to his past, but every time he pushed her away, he felt as though he was peeling away his own skin.

Even so, this obsession with her *had* to stop.

CHAPTER EIGHT

Siobhan had a restless night. She tossed and turned, reliving how Joaquin had been so antagonistic about Ramon. Jealous?

That was what she'd thought when he'd declared so angrily, *I care.*

He had startled her enough that she'd spilled her guts over how badly she'd misjudged Gilbert and his feelings toward her.

Joaquin had seemed so kind, then. He'd sounded as though he really did care.

Flowing into his embrace had felt as natural as it had every other time. And she ought to know by now that an explosion of passion would happen, but it had caught her off guard, being even more powerful than she expected. She would have made love with him in his office! Anyone could have walked in on them.

She covered her hot face thinking of her abandonment and the way that he had put such a cold stop to it, as though he was barely affected at all.

He didn't care. Not really. Not the way she longed for someone to care about her.

Once again, she was fooling herself into seeing what she wanted to see.

To hell with him, she resolved as she dressed for work. She had tried to make it clear to him that she needed to support herself financially because she didn't feel right leaning on people she'd let down. She resented how he was making her ability to do so seem *impossible*.

She jerked her brush through her hair hard enough to bring tears to her eyes, gathering it in a low ponytail as if it was Casual Friday when it was only Tuesday.

She had a *plan*. A few weeks from the end of this mat cover, she would start looking for an entry-level management position. Maybe in Miami, she thought spitefully, even though her sister's life there was very WAG-centric with lots of hours devoted to hair and nails and parties as she kept up with the trends set by the other wives and girlfriends of the athletes.

Those athletes had a lot of money, though, and there were a lot of contracts for sponsorships that needed a sharp eye to dot i's and cross t's.

Alternately, she could move back to London and find something in banking or insurance. Or try San Francisco again. Programmers were a dime a dozen, but a lot of them worked on contract. There was a ton of opportunity for her there.

Now that she was gaining experience in acquisition at this tech company, she would be an even stronger candidate there.

So yes, Joaquin, I need this job, she silently shouted across the city at him.

She refused, absolutely refused, to let him jeopardize it.

Not that she brought her best game to the office when she finally got there. She felt hungover, nursing a vague nausea that she blamed on her lack of sleep.

When are you arriving? her sister texted midmorning. The children are asking.

She ignored Cinnia's message, feeling too overwhelmed to think about Christmas when she still needed to get through the week.

And the staff party, she was reminded when someone came around collecting final numbers.

"Are you bringing a date?" they asked.

A wicked vision of Joaquin flashed in her mind. Would he ask her to dance? *Oh, stop it*, she scolded herself. What was she? Twelve? Ugh.

"I haven't even found something to wear," she replied, wishing she could bow out altogether, but these sorts of events were valuable networking opportunities. She would push through.

"We're needed upstairs," Oladele said, arriving at her desk to interrupt them.

Siobhan smiled a weak apology and gathered her things, accompanying Oladele to the elevator.

"You seem pale today," Oladele noted. "Are you unwell?"

"It's this color." She plucked at the mustard-toned pullover. "I should give it away because it washes me out, but it's one of my comfort wears." The thick, soft knit felt like a hug.

"I have a cardigan like that. It's full of holes. I can't leave the house in it, but I refuse to throw it away."

They continued joking about their reluctance to break up with favorite clothing until they walked into the boardroom.

Joaquin was already there with several other people. His gaze swept over her in a way that scraped at her composure.

Siobhan sobered and averted her eyes, heart squeezed by the vise of her behavior yesterday.

No more, she resolved as she took her seat behind Oladele and opened her laptop, preparing to take notes. She might respond to him physically, but that was a trick of chemistry that meant nothing. She was setting higher standards for herself.

They were *over*.

Joaquin had steeled himself against so much as looking at Siobhan when she arrived for the meeting, but his damned inner radar had heard her voice approaching and turned his head.

Now, as he quickly ran through the agenda, making swift decisions around reallocating resources, all he could see was lipstick the color of pink gelato against a pale complexion, a chunky yellow knit clinging to narrow shoulders, and breasts he'd caressed as recently as yesterday.

The tension in his abdomen, and lower, came out in his voice.

"Where are we at with the defamation charges?" he

asked Oladele, stubbornly keeping his gaze on her, not the stony, downcast face behind her.

"I was going to chase that this morning, but was sidetracked by a complaint lodged against me at the General Council's office," Oladele said.

"By who?" he bit out.

"It was anonymous," Oladele said with an annoyed shake of her head. "But I'm sure we can guess who's behind it."

"He does not come after my staff," Joaquin gritted out, infuriated by how petty Lorenzo was. He had no compunction against destroying innocent people if he could score a point against his son.

See? he wanted to say to Siobhan. *This is what I'm shielding you from.*

"Stay behind after this," he ordered Oladele and quickly wrapped up the rest.

"Do you need me?" Siobhan asked Oladele, gathering her laptop and notebook into her arms as everyone else filed out.

"No," Joaquin answered.

Siobhan flinched at his tone and flashed him a glance then haughtily turned her gaze on Oladele.

He kicked himself, especially when Oladele sent him a look of surprise as well before she answered Siobhan. "Head back to your desk. I'll be down shortly."

Siobhan nodded and moved to the door.

Joaquin took a single long stride to get it for her, feeling like a heel, wanting to at least catch her eye and let her know he hadn't meant to be so rude.

If he hadn't been right there, staring at her profile, he

would have missed the way the rigidity left it and her eyelashes fluttered. He would have missed how her color leached away and her knees buckled. He wouldn't have been close enough to catch her before she hit the floor.

"Wha—?" His heart lodged itself in his mouth as her dead weight slumped in his arms. Her laptop hit the carpet and her notebook splashed open.

Oladele gasped.

"Call first aid," he barked.

Since he'd caught her and knew she wasn't injured, Joaquin gathered Siobhan against his chest. "Get the door. I'll put her on the sofa in my office."

Seconds later, he eased her onto the cushions, heart crashing against the walls of his rib cage. Her eyes were already blinking open.

"What—?"

"You fainted." He had rudimentary first aid knowledge and pulled her eyelids up to ensure her pupils were even, then pressed his fingertips to the pulse in her throat.

"First aid is on their way," Oladele said from the door. "Do we need an ambulance?"

"*No.* I just stood up too fast." Siobhan brushed his hands off her and sat up, forcing him to rise so she could set her feet on the floor.

He touched her shoulder to keep her seated, ready to catch her if she slumped forward.

"I don't need first aid," she said impatiently. "That's embarrassing. I'm fine."

"You are not. You were dizzy the other day." Joaquin had let himself believe her when she had said it was a bug, even though a tiny seed of suspicion had arrived in his brain at the time, one he had dismissed before he allowed it to take root. It was too perilous. It would consume his thoughts if he let it, so he had brushed it away.

It was quickly growing too big to ignore, though. Or would. Over the next nine months.

No. He pinched the bridge of his nose, still wanting to believe it was something else.

"Do you have a headache?" He didn't want her to be genuinely ill, but it was the only other explanation. "A cough? Other symptoms?"

"No."

"I wish you had told me you weren't feeling well." Oladele flicked Joaquin a look of speculation that only landed on him long enough to blow up his shell of denial before she returned her concerned frown on Siobhan. She suspected the same thing, but she was too circumspect to say it aloud. "I don't fire people for being ill, even if they're new on the job."

"I didn't think you would. But I'm not sick," Siobhan insisted. "This is self-induced. I've been burning the candle at both ends."

"Did you miss lunch again?" Oladele asked.

"You've been skipping lunch?" Joaquin snapped before she could answer.

"A couple of times on those first days. Things were busy. You're both overreacting."

On the contrary, he'd been underreacting. Refusing to see what was blatantly obvious.

Damn it, *he* was starting to feel faint. There was a

buzz in his ears and he couldn't find any oxygen in this damned dungeon of an office.

"I insist you take better care of yourself," Oladele was saying. "I'll fetch your things. I want you to start your Christmas break immediately. See a doctor as soon as you can, then let me know if you need more time off. Otherwise, I'll see you in the New Year, back in fighting form." Oladele opened the door. "Ah. Here's first aid." She let in a young man wearing a red cross on his sleeve. "I'll be back in a moment."

Oladele left and the young man asked permission to check Siobhan's vitals before he applied a blood pressure cuff to her arm and used a stethoscope against her inner elbow.

"This is very unnecessary," she complained to Joaquin.

He pointed at the phone against his ear. The receptionist at the clinic had just picked up. He advised her that he was bringing his colleague for an assessment.

"We'll be there in thirty minutes," he said before ending the call.

"I can book my own doctor," Siobhan said with annoyance. "No, I'm not diabetic," she replied to the first aid attendant who was running through a checklist. "No, no, no," she continued.

"Pregnant?"

"N—*oh.*" Her reply came out a lot less certain. Her voice actually cracked. She began to blush. Deeply. She shot a stark look at Joaquin.

She really hadn't suspected? Because in his mind it had become as impossible to miss as a five-alarm fire.

He was already down the road of how he would shield her from his father's machinations while questioning his own fitness as a father. He had never wanted to face these sorts of dilemmas. That was why he used common sense and condoms.

"I apologize." The attendant misinterpreted her embarrassment. "These are personal questions. I shouldn't be asking them in front of anyone else. Would you excuse us, señor?"

"The clinic is holding a spot for her," Joaquin said crisply. "You can cut this short. I'll take her there myself."

"I can do that if—" the young man started to offer.

"No," Joaquin said.

"Of course." The young man kept his speculations to himself as he repacked his bag, telling Siobhan, "Your vitals are normal, but shall I bring the wheelchair?"

"No. Thank you." She still sounded strangled.

She refused to look at Joaquin, remaining stoic as Oladele arrived with her things.

Joaquin helped her put on her coat, then took her bag. Her expression remained stiff and unreadable as they left his office.

He heard her thoughts all the same. They echoed his own.

This can't happen.

No, no, no. There were a million reasons she couldn't be pregnant, especially by Joaquin. He was her *boss*. They barely knew each other. They had only had sex once. He had worn a condom.

There was no way she could be pregnant.

She accompanied him to the elevator anyway, blaming the roil in her stomach on nerves. It had to be nerves. But why was she nervous if there was nothing to worry about?

"Have you been with anyone else?" he asked when the doors of the elevator enclosed them into privacy.

"No." Her heart lurched as though the car was freefalling. "Have *you*?"

"No," he said coolly. "And I didn't think you had, but I thought I should ask."

For some reason, his question made it more real. More likely. Her eyes grew hot. It became impossible to draw a full breath.

"What will we do if—" Her voice broke.

"Let's wait to see if there's anything to talk about before we talk," he said in that same grave, detached tone.

She caught back a panicked sob and nodded, for once bolstered by his air of cool command. She let him escort her across the lobby, ignoring the stares from the handful of employees who recognized them. She must look like death. She felt as though she walked through sticky molasses.

They were both quiet in the car. She didn't know what he might be thinking behind his remote expression. She didn't have room in her turmoiled thoughts to imagine it. She just kept trying to blame these symptoms on all the stress she'd been under. It was flu season. Sometimes she felt off when she was expecting her cycle. That was all this was. It had to be!

She knew it wasn't, though. She knew.

The moment they entered the reception lounge, before she even saw the doctor, she asked for a sample cup and took it to the toilet.

She went into the examination room alone and the doctor came in a few minutes later to introduce himself.

"Your suspicion is correct," he said with calm professionalism.

"But I had a period." She barely got the words out, her mouth was so dry.

"Typical? Or lighter than normal?"

"Light." Barely spotting, but it had been right on time. She had blamed all the travel and time changes for it finishing before it had properly started.

She wanted to fold in on herself for being so naive. For not understanding that was why she was so tired. She'd been around dozens of pregnancies over the years. She should have recognized when it happened to her.

It hadn't occurred to her because she wasn't ready to be a mother. She didn't even have the sense to notice she was about to become one!

Was she really going to be a mother? Her heart was beating so fast, she had to wonder if she was going to make it through the end of the day. She tried to imagine what her life would look like with a baby and all she saw was a white void where her job and apartment and career ambitions had been.

Distantly, she heard the doctor prescribe prenatal vitamins and mention the need for a physical and a scan and ongoing prenatal checkups "if you choose to continue to term."

Her heart lurched. She had always planned to have a family, just not yet. Not alone.

What would Joaquin even say?

Let's wait to see if there's anything to talk about before we talk.

Reason one million that I don't want children.

Her hands were icy as she gathered her handbag and returned to the waiting area.

Joaquin was still on his feet and turned from the window. He flinched when he saw her expression and wordlessly held her coat.

In the elevator, she said, "We have something to talk about."

He nodded curtly and escorted her into his car.

She didn't pay attention to where he took her, not until they arrived at an unfamiliar building.

"Where are we?" she asked numbly as he helped her step onto the sidewalk.

"My apartment. The security is excellent and my father has a town house in Salamanca. You don't have to worry he'll turn up here."

Lorenzo was the last thing she was worried about. Joaquin hadn't beamed with joy and hugged her when she gave him the news. He had retreated another thousand miles inside himself.

She had an impression of marble columns and a polite door staff as they entered. Like many public spaces this time of year, the lobby was decked with twinkling lights and scalloped ribbons interspersed with bells. A beautiful nativity scene with hand-painted figurines stood on a table between a pair of elevators.

Joaquin used his thumbprint to access a panel. Seconds later, they entered a penthouse that had been modernized while keeping much of the building's heritage charm.

He waved her into the living room where a tree sparkled with white lights. Flames danced in the gas fireplace.

"This is Marta, my housekeeper," he said of the middle-aged woman who emerged from the kitchen to smile in greeting. "Thank you for staying late, Marta. This is Ms. Upton."

"*Buenas*—um, *noches*?" Siobhan had lost track of time. There was still a glimmer of fading dusk beyond the windows, but she felt as though a week had passed since she'd fainted at work.

"Welcome," Marta said in warm Spanish. "May I take your coats? I've prepared a light meal if you'd like me to serve it?"

"I texted her that you missed lunch." Joaquin seated her at the dining table where freshly baked buns gave off a heavenly aroma. Candles wreathed in holly sat on the table, lending a gentle festive atmosphere.

"That's not why I fainted," Siobhan said when Marta was in the kitchen. "The doctor said it's not uncommon for blood pressure to fall in—" she had to clear her throat, still wrapping her head around it. "—in early pregnancy. He said he'd test my iron levels when I go back for bloodwork, to be sure I'm not anemic."

Marta brought out bowls of *pescado en blanco*. It was a light soup that Siobhan already knew would sit gently in her unsettled stomach.

"I've kept you late enough," Joaquin said when Marta asked if she could bring them anything else. "We'll manage. Enjoy your evening."

"*Gracias, señor.* I'll clean the dishes in the morning." Marta wished them good-night and left.

"I feel like all you do is feed me," Siobhan said as she tucked into her soup.

"If you would feed yourself, I wouldn't have to, would I?"

She was so on edge, she flinched.

They ate in subdued silence.

"So, um…" Siobhan couldn't stand the suspense any longer. "Still a skeptic about fate?"

It was a terrible joke. He didn't reveal one glimmer of amusement.

"We both have free will here. Your choices will affect mine so, ladies first."

Her veins stung with heightened emotion. This was sooner than she had planned to start her family and she had always imagined she would be in a loving, committed relationship when she did, but "I'm having the baby."

CHAPTER NINE

Her voice was quiet, the words simple, but they hit Joaquin with the force of a hurricane wind, nearly knocking him from his chair.

She was having the baby. *They* were having a baby.

The world titled on its axis. He resisted the urge to grip the table as he felt himself falling into empty space.

Conflicting responses warred within him. A desire to backtrack. If he could return to that elevator in San Francisco, he would go to his room alone— But no. A resistance rose in him even as he considered giving up that memory. It was too good.

Let the doctor be mistaken and I'll... What? What could he do to atone for getting a woman pregnant?

"You're not happy." She pushed aside her empty bowl and walked to the fireplace where she stood with her back to him, hunched, hugging herself. "It's okay. I'm making this decision for me. I want to be a mother. I'm not doing it lightly, either." She turned her head to speak over her shoulder, offering him the curve of a cheek carved from ivory. "I've been around a lot of pregnant women and their children. I know what I'm in for more than most first-time mothers. I have a ton of support and resources. You don't have to be involved."

"Stop." He left his own chair and walked around the sofa toward her. "I've never wanted to be a parent, that's true. It doesn't mean I intend to ignore the fact I'm about to become one." *I am one.* The fist around his lungs clenched tighter.

"But no one needs to know that. Most couples don't tell anyone about their pregnancy in the first trimester anyway, in case something goes wrong. We can keep pretending we're merely acquainted—"

"No." He didn't let her finish, offended on a very primal level that she would even suggest he turn his back on both of them.

Something very visceral was springing to life in him that he didn't want to examine too closely. It was greedy and atavistic and protective and it wouldn't be pushed to the margins where his actions would be ineffective.

"Why have you never wanted children?" She pleated her brow in anxious incomprehension.

He winced and reached for the most obvious explanation.

"I travel too much. They're a level of responsibility that always seemed inconvenient." He loosened his tie, feeling constricted by it. "One of the reasons my brother and I struggled to reconnect was the fact he had young children. His family was his priority. Which was as it should be, but I saw how much of his time they monopolized."

He pushed his hands into his pockets, still trying to wrap his head around this news while that belief, that personal *standard* of his brother's, settled into him as his own. His priorities had been shuffled. New ones had arrived at the top in the form of Siobhan and their child.

"I am responsible for this baby, though. I refuse to shirk that."

"That's admirable, Joaquin, but a child needs to feel like more than an obligation." Her chin stayed low with admonishment as she lifted her lashes. "You need to *want* to be a parent. With me." Her voice wavered toward hysterical laughter. "For twenty years. This is a big decision for you, too. *You* can take more time to think on it."

Her pregnancy wasn't even visible. The idea they would be linked by this unformed person for the rest of their lives was something too big to grasp. The profound weakness a baby would create for him was terrifying to comprehend, but there was also a strange allure in this news.

A glimmer of something arrived in him. It was akin to what he'd seen in Fernando when his brother had introduced him to his firstborn, looping his arm around Zurina, who had been holding the baby. The pride in his brother's expression had been so blatant, Joaquin had been embarrassed for him, but he could feel emotion dawning in his chest.

"The deed is done," he said. "I *am* a father. If you're asking how I intend to behave as one, the answer is, *better than the example that was set for me.*"

As he made that decision, and this new reality began to settle on him, his mind raced ahead to reconfigure his future around both of them.

* * *

"I appreciate you saying that." Siobhan sank with profound relief onto the edge of the sofa cushion, elbows on her knees, fingers laced before her unsteady lips.

The truth was she was moved by how quickly and firmly he was committing to their baby. It meant a lot to her.

"I was raised by a single mom. I don't have qualms about being one. I know the part that really matters is having someone who loves you." Even if she had faced raising their baby alone, she would have had a ton of help from her mother and sisters. "All of my sisters remember our father except me. I was a toddler when he died. It left a blank space that Henri did his best to fill, but he didn't come into my life until I was in my teens. Then I saw what a loving, involved father he is to their children and I've always known I wanted that for my own. So thank you."

"For not leaving a blank space in our own baby's life? You're welcome, I guess."

Our own baby.

Her shock was wearing off. Anticipation gathered in her chest and thickened in her throat. Joy expanded through her, creating room for the new love that was blooming inside her. What would their child be like? Moody and watchful like Joaquin? Aloof? Or affectionate and cheeky like her?

She let herself picture Joaquin with an infant against his heart and was nearly overwhelmed by longing. Would their baby bring out a warmth in him he didn't otherwise reveal? Or was she conjuring a romantic illusion?

Henri hadn't wanted children when he and Cinnia had started their affair. Cinnia had broken things off with him when she discovered her pregnancy, then hid it from him for months, even though they'd been in a relationship for two years. Even though they'd been in love, whether they had admitted it to themselves or not.

Her situation with Joaquin was very different, Siobhan acknowledged with a pang of chilling clarity. She and Joaquin were essentially strangers. They had slept together once. They had a few conversations between them that had been very personal on her side, but there was a lot she didn't know about him. She didn't have any of the confidence in his feelings that Cinnia had had about Henri's. In fact, all he'd done was shut her down.

For all she knew, Joaquin was only stepping up because of her relationship to Henri and the rest of the Sauveterres. He was a practical, tactical man. He had to recognize that, on a social level, having a baby with her would tie him into their circles forever.

And she was liable to let him! From the moment she had seen him again, she had been fighting her desire to be physically intimate with him again. To feel once more his masterful stroking of her body, the exquisite spikes of pleasure he brought forth, the culmination and blissful aftermath.

He didn't truly care for her, though. He might be decent enough to catch her when she fainted and show concern over the baby he'd put in her, but he wasn't as affected by her as she was by him. His ability to cool things off between them again and again proved it.

Which made her worry she would fall further under his spell if she didn't keep a firm distance.

"Okay, so, um, that's good to know that you're, you know, committed. I'll keep you posted as I make decisions." She rose and found her handbag. "Is your driver still on the clock? Or should I order my own car?"

His dark brows quirked in astonished puzzlement. "To where?"

"Home. Wait. Is it still rush hour?" She glanced toward the windows where city lights were sprinkled against the dark night. "Maybe I'll take the metro."

"You fainted today." His tone said, *remember*?

"Right. Car, then." She brought her phone from her purse.

"Siobhan. You're not going home. You'll stay here where I can keep an eye on you."

"I'm not going home to paint the ceiling. I'll put my feet up, have an early night. But I *have* to go home to take out these contacts. They feel like sandpaper." She blinked as she tried to read her screen, growing desperate for time alone to regroup and come to terms with all of this.

"Don't order a car," he said with impatience. "I'll take you home." He came to hold her coat for her. "You can pack what you need to move in with me."

CHAPTER TEN

"What? I can't move in with you!"

"Why not?" Joaquin asked the question, but then held up a finger as he brought his phone to his ear.

She stewed while he spoke to his driver.

"He's happy to collect overtime." He ended the call. "He'll meet us downstairs in a few minutes."

"What on earth makes you think I want to move in with you?" she cried.

"Your tone?" he suggested drily as he pulled on his own overcoat.

"Why would you even want me to?" she demanded. The belt on her coat felt too tight.

"Half the building saw us leave together today. I would love to believe I've ferreted out all the moles, but rumors are liable to get back to my father. I won't underestimate what he might do with that information. You can't work there, not while he's still trying to reclaim it."

"You're not firing me." She put her foot down.

"No, I'm protecting you," he said in his most implacable tone. "You heard today how he's going after Oladele." He muttered a distracted curse and rubbed his jaw. "I still have to deal with that. But he could target you just as ruthlessly."

"So I should lie down and let him quash my career before I've properly got it off the ground?"

He glowered at her.

She lifted her chin and gave him a too-sweet smile. "Yeah. It turns out I'm smart enough to see the holes in your logic."

"As your employer," he said very patronizingly, "and the father of your unborn child, I *insist* you stay off work until you have your health in order. *Then* we will discuss if and where you can work." Oh, he was smug over that.

"I'll make my own decisions, thank you very much."

"Then make smart ones!" He opened the door.

"How does quitting my job and moving in with you serve me in any way?"

"We just agreed we're doing this together." He nodded at her middle. "How does that happen if I'm in Barcelona and you're here? Because as soon as this acquisition is finalized, I'm finding a new CEO for LVG and will only be here quarterly."

"And you expect me to pick up sticks and go to Barcelona with you? For how long?"

"Twenty years?" he replied, shrugging.

"You're unbelievable."

The driver arrived at the curb as they exited the building. Siobhan got into the car because she had a feeling Joaquin would have the driver take him to her building regardless.

After ten minutes of stewing in bumper-to-bumper traffic, she leaned forward to ask the driver if he spoke English.

"No, señora," he said with an apologetic shake of his head.

"No problem," she assured him in Spanish. "Please disregard any raised voices you hear in the next few minutes."

The driver chuckled and Siobhan switched to English.

"You don't get to order me to quit my job and move in with you," she hissed.

"What are you? A vampire? You're *invited*."

"To be what?" she challenged. "Your houseguest? Are we going from pretending *not* to be a couple to pretending to *be* a couple? Will we be roommates who coparent or are you *inviting* me—" she wrapped the word in a layer of sarcasm "—to start a relationship with you?"

He seemed to retreat a little more into the shadowed backseat. "We're already in a relationship."

"Hardly." He ignored her more often than he spoke to her.

"You're asking if I want to have sex with you?" he growled. "I think I proved that yesterday."

A choked noise of embarrassed skepticism left her.

"Again, I was protecting *you*. The door wasn't locked," he reminded her through his teeth. "I don't care who sees my ass. I'd happily finish what we started right here, right now, but you fainted today so sex is off the table."

Her pulse skipped at the lewd image he painted. She almost told him the doctor hadn't said she couldn't have sex, but she refused to beg for crumbs from him.

"What I'm hearing is you want me to move in with you, be a mother to your child and conveniently sleep with you. Essentially, be a wife without being your wife."

"We can talk about marriage," he said with a note of surprise. "I'm open to it."

"We don't even know each other! A few weeks ago, you made it clear you weren't interested in sharing anything more than one night. Not even that," she reminded hotly. "So excuse me if I don't rush to move in with a man who might want his baby, but doesn't really want *me*."

He did want her, though. It was torturing him how much he wanted her because he had learned to only care about the things he needed. He would battle to the death over food and air. Sleep was a necessity, but a comfortable bed was a want. Sharing a bed with *her* was...

An old, twisting sensation went through him, the one that reminded him not to reveal his wants. Wanting her meant exposing a flank. It meant putting her in the line of fire. And their baby? He could hardly stand how vulnerable that made him.

Yet, a dark part of him was pleased her pregnancy forced him to bring her more fully into his life.

"I wasn't prepared to start something long-term when I met you. Not with all of this going on with my father. A relationship would have been a distraction. But now..."

He sensed her head turn. She was listening attentively.

"I know I'm difficult to read. You're not the first woman to say so, but I don't like people to know what I'm thinking or feeling. That's not comfortable for me."

"It's not comfortable for anyone," she said impatiently, tucking her chin on her palm and her elbow on the armrest as she looked out her side window. "But at least tell me..." She dropped her hands into her lap. "Is that the only reason you gave me the brush-off that night? Or..."

"What?" he prompted.

"It's not that long since you were engaged. Was I a rebound from that?"

"No." The car stopped. He stepped out to put an end to the conversation.

His driver opened her door and Joaquin arrived on the sidewalk in time to offer his hand as she rose from the car.

"Thank you," she said stiffly. "But you don't have to walk me in. We can talk tomorrow." She nodded at the car as though dismissing him.

Did she really think she could out-stubborn him? "You're not spending the night alone. Not until you've had all the bloodwork and whatnot from the doctor."

"What are you going to do? Stare at me while I sleep? Because I don't see a point in spending time with you if you refuse to talk to me."

"I'm not refusing." Just avoiding certain uncomfortable topics. "We're staying here tonight," he told his driver. "Come back for me at seven tomorrow morning."

Siobhan huffed a noise of muted outrage and started toward the front doors.

"What exactly do you want to know?" he asked reluctantly as he caught up to her.

She paused with her key fob in her hand, surprise in

her expression. "About your engagement? What was her name? How did you meet her?"

"Esperanza. She works in real estate. She found my penthouse in Barcelona for me."

"Why did you break up?"

"My father." He took the fob from her loose grip and waved it at the sensor, then held the door. "I wasn't involved in LVG when I proposed, but after Fernando passed, I came here to support Zurina through the funeral. My father assumed I was here to fight him for LVG and turned his spite onto Esperanza."

"In what way?" She wasn't watching where she was going. She was looking at him so he took her elbow as he led her to the elevator.

"Insults. Tantrums," he said tiredly. "Veiled threats. Nothing illegal. He's very clever that way. And manipulative. When I called him out on his behavior and ordered him from Zurina's home, he accused me of trying to prevent him from seeing his grandchildren. I couldn't be around him without wanting to strangle him. That's how he got Zurina to allow him to take over at LVG. She was trying to keep the peace and lived to regret it. He still saw me as a threat, though, and began interfering in Esperanza's real estate deals. She said she couldn't marry me if it meant losing her livelihood. I couldn't abandon Zurina so I agreed we should break it off."

"I think *I* mentioned not wanting to lose my livelihood," she muttered as they stepped into the elevator. "Are you…still in love with her?"

"No."

"*Were* you?"

"No."

"Really?" Her eyes flared wide with surprise. "Then why were you planning to spend your life with her?"

"Compatibility?" He shrugged.

"You mean…in bed?" she asked warily.

Dios, she was persistent.

"She didn't want children," he said flatly.

Siobhan took a sharp breath, staggering back a step.

"I'm being frank so you don't think I'm harboring secrets." The doors opened and he held them for her. "Esperanza has a likable personality and she's very career focused. Marriage was never a goal for me, but after we'd been seeing each other for a year, she asked if I intended to propose. We were comfortable, so I did."

"She wasn't in love, either?"

Here he vacillated before telling the truth. "She said she was," he admitted. "That's another reason I didn't fight her leaving. I didn't want to lead her on."

Siobhan stopped at her door, expression deeply vulnerable.

"I'm not built for that sort of depth," he admitted with a wince, feeling as though he stood on quicksand. He felt *inadequate*. But it was best to make that clear to her now. "I promise to be a good partner to you, though. I will support you. I will protect you."

Her brows pulled with uncertainty as she took back her fob and opened her door, striding in ahead of him.

He followed, coming up short as he saw her flat had been overturned.

* * *

As she reached for the door on the closet, Joaquin caught her arm and scooped her behind him, corralling her against the door to the hall.

"What—?"

"Leave. Go to your neighbor's. He might still be here."

"Who?" Her fists instinctively closed in the folds of his coat.

"Whoever searched the place. I'm calling the police!" he called out, reaching into his pocket. "He's gone too far this time," he added in a mutter of barely contained rage.

She peered around him into her silent flat, glimpsing the chaos of wrapping paper, ribbons and unwrapped toys. Nothing else looked amiss.

"Wait," she said sheepishly. "I left it like this."

His shoulders dropped. He angled to look down on her, astounded.

"I've been trying to do the wrapping all week." Acute embarrassment rose in her. She walked into the mess and discarded her coat over a chair, kicking off her shoes. "I told you it was Christmas when Ramon told me what Gilbert had done. I was actually wrapping gifts." She waved hopelessly at the wrapping paper she had unrolled across her dining table. A train set was centered on it. Tape, scissors, ribbons and labels were scattered next to it. "I used to love this time of year. Now it stresses me out. That's the real reason I don't have a tree. Christmas is ruined for me."

He frowned. "What have you been doing since it happened?"

"Asking Mom and my sisters to join me in Australia."

She pulled her shoulders up defensively. "It feels different there. It's summer. We kept it no gifts and went snorkeling or had a barbecue. I didn't have to face it. But Cinnia will have all the children there this year. I couldn't say no. I *want* to be there, but also…" She clutched her stomach. Her chest felt tight.

"This is genuinely difficult for you." He came across to rub her arms and frown at her.

"It is." She grimaced at the sheer volume of the task ahead. "I feel so silly for reacting like this, but each time I try to do it, I just *can't*."

"I'll do it." He wasn't laughing at her, which kind of made her feel extra wobbly inside. "Remove your contacts or whatever it was you needed to do."

"*You're* not going to wrap all these gifts," she said with disbelief.

"I am." He released her and shifted the train set on the paper. He lifted the roll to better estimate how much was needed then picked up the scissors and slid them in a smooth hiss, cutting a precise line.

"Do you like it?"

"I don't mind it." He knew what he was doing, too. He was economical and very tidy, keeping everything square, folding edges for clean lines, tucking and taping with smooth expertise. "The first component I manufactured was a type of gaming goggles. My initial order was two thousand. I sold out in three days, partly because I promised to gift wrap them. Do you know how many employees I had at the time?"

She shook her head, bemused.

"One. Me."

"Really?" A smile tugged at her lips, picturing him both proud and overwhelmed by his own success.

"I had to become very good, very fast." He pulled a stretch of ribbon from the roll and wrapped it in jaunty angles around the corners of the gift. He tied it off and, with a quick zip-zip of the scissor blades, bounced a few curlicues into the tails. He topped it with a bow and offered it to her. "Santa's helper unlocked."

It was beautiful.

And it was such a kind gesture, she thought she might cry.

CHAPTER ELEVEN

JOAQUIN HADN'T DONE anything so menial in years, but it was worth it for the bright smile it put on Siobhan's face. It felt good to do something concrete for her, especially when she kept yawning so hard.

"Go to bed," he urged. "I'll join you when I'm done."

"I love how you assume you're invited to sleep with me."

"If you want to go back to my place, I have a guest room," he said mildly.

"Tsk." She stood in the opening to her bedroom, a truculent look on her face. She had changed into yoga pants and a tunic and adjusted her glasses before catching another yawn in her cupped hand.

"I would offer to tuck you in, but you're too tired for sex. Go to sleep. We can argue as much as you want tomorrow. Promise."

"Generous of you," she muttered, but a few minutes later she closed the bedroom doors and the lights went out.

Two hours later, he stripped to his briefs and carefully settled beside her. Her bed was only a queen so he was close enough to feel her body heat.

"Joaquin?" she murmured sleepily as she rolled toward him.

"Are you expecting someone else?"

She gave a muted hum of amusement. "Thank you for doing the wrapping. I really appreciate it." Her warm, silky hand found his upper arm, waking the animal in him.

"De nada." He rolled to face her, tucking his arm under his pillow while catching her hand and bringing it to his lips. "Are you awake or going back to sleep?"

"I—" She drew her hand out of his. "I'm afraid to move in with you," she admitted in a whisper.

His heart swerved. "Why?"

"Because then we'll do that. And I might fall in love with you. I don't want you to propose one day because I make you feel like you have to and you only do it because we're comfortable."

Ouch. He fell onto his back again.

"I'm sorry. That came out harsher than I meant it to."

"It's fine." Fair. "Go to sleep."

"You're angry."

"No." Not at her. He was angry at himself and his own limitations.

She rolled away and exhaled.

He stared at the ceiling, trying to see his way through this because the irony was, if he ever proposed, it would be *in spite of the fact* he wasn't comfortable with her. Siobhan had been disrupting his life and his peace of mind from the beginning. Even before learning about the baby, he'd been unable to forget her. He found her interesting and smart and funny.

Now the baby was upending his entire existence and he ought to be furious, but he couldn't find it in him to be sorry. That was what he was thinking as he closed his eyes. *I'm not sorry.*

His subconscious reminded him why he should be, though. As reality folded into the dream world, Lorenzo's true nature lurched into his psyche.

That's not for you. Only Fernando may have that.

In the way of muddled dreams, an old memory was rewritten. Siobhan was *there*. Lorenzo's arm was swinging, but not toward Joaquin.

"Siobhan!" he shouted, waking with a jolt to an unfamiliar place and movement beside him as she sat up, gasping.

"It's okay." He searched out her wrist, keeping her on the bed so she wouldn't flee into the shadows and trip.

His throat was still rasped by his shout, his chest tight with adrenaline, his skin clammy. The disturbing images of his dream stuck like cobwebs that he mentally had to brush away.

"Did you have a nightmare?" She sank onto the mattress beside him. Her hand arrived on his chest while the rest of her aligned along his side. "Your heart is racing. Are you okay?"

"Fine," he lied while he fought the urge to loop his arm around her and hug her against his tacky skin.

He was too raw for that. Too involved, if he was reacting with this much terror to his own imagined threats.

"I didn't mean to wake you." He pressed her away. "Go back to sleep."

"But—" She sat up again as he left the bed. "It's still early. You need to sleep, too."

"I'll check email. There will be some from overseas that need answering." It was a fib, but he needed to regroup. He picked up his trousers and stepped into them.

In the lounge, he looked at his phone, but his mind wouldn't focus.

Work had always been a productive coping mechanism. As a child, he had used homework and invention to avoid his father's criticism and attempt to earn his recognition. Later, he had labored to afford food and a place to sleep, but it had kept him from dwelling on how alone he felt. Once he had had more of a financial toehold, he had toiled feverishly to surpass his father's level of success, so he could no longer be victimized by Lorenzo. When that was achieved, he continued to strive as a point of pride. Out of spite, even, so he could look down on Lorenzo.

I won, was the silent message he had conveyed with the rise of ProFab into worldwide acclaim.

But had he? Lorenzo was still able to invade his dreams and leave the bitter taste of copper on the back of his tongue.

"Joaquin?"

Her voice pierced between his shoulder blades. He turned to see her in a blue robe wearing a worried expression.

"You said you'd start looking after yourself," he chided.

"I can't sleep. Not when you're having nightmares about…" She waved toward the knotted belt on the robe.

"That wasn't what it was about."

"What, then?"

"It doesn't matter."

She came closer and searched his expression in the dim light. "The stress of becoming a father brought it on, though. Are you having second thoughts?"

He wanted to deflect, walk away, close off. Anything to avoid this, but he answered her. "I'm not afraid to be a father," he blurted. "I'm afraid for *you*."

"Why?"

He scrubbed his stubble with his palm. The nightmare had been an icy, subliminal warning of what could happen if Joaquin wasn't vigilant.

"The dream was about my father."

"And me?" She closed the robe tighter across her chest with her fist. "But it was just a dream, Joaquin. Wasn't it? Joaquin, was he…abusive?" she asked in a whisper.

"Yes."

Her breath hissed in. "Physically? Your ribs?"

"Yes."

"Where were the authorities?" she asked with anguish. "Why wasn't he stopped?"

"He told the doctors I'd jumped from the hayloft. Boys will be boys."

"Your mother?"

"She had already left."

"And left you with him?" She started toward him.

He put up a hand, holding her off. He couldn't bear her tenderness right now.

"She didn't know. Not until later. Don't blame her. I

was questioned, but I was worried I'd be separated from Fernando so I didn't tell them the truth."

"I don't understand how people can be like that. Especially to a child." She covered her mouth with her hand.

"I asked my mother once if I was the product of an affair, thinking that might explain why he was so petty toward me. I was barely old enough to understand that people could have affairs, but I wanted my father to be someone else. Desperately," he said on a scuff of a laugh. "She said he was just a mean, small, jealous man. He was," he said with contempt. "He was horribly jealous of his own brother. LVG was bequeathed to both of them and they fought over it until my uncle died. That's one of the reasons Lorenzo always made sure I knew Fernando was the heir and I the spare."

"But when Fernando died…?" Her brow was knotted with incomprehension, her chin crinkled.

"Jealous again. Of me." He lifted a hand and a defeated breath left him. "I think that's part of it. He's always seen me as a threat on some level, stealing attention or questioning him or pushing back on his bad ideas. Fernando and I were close growing up, despite his efforts to divide us. Maybe I just reminded him of his brother. I don't know, but it came to a head when I was fourteen and designed a relay component. We lived and breathed electronics growing up. In that way, I had a very privileged life."

"Not if he was abusive."

He looked away, trying to ignore the slash of pain that went through his chest. The wave of old helplessness that wanted to swallow him.

"In any case, I had the brain of an engineer and handed my father the schematic. I guess I thought if I earned his respect, things would change. It was the logic of a child. Of..." Wanting to be loved. Or at least accepted.

Siobhan was listening closely, searching his expression.

He swallowed. "It allowed LVG to become a leader in that pocket of the market. Two years later, I could see that it was a success. I wanted him to acknowledge that I had done something useful for LVG. That I was an asset. That's all." He was still baffled by his father's reaction. "I wasn't asking for money, only for him to say I had done a good job. He called me a liar, claimed he had designed it himself and threw me from the house." He could still feel his father's fist in his hair. The propulsion out the door. The gravel hitting his knees and palms. He could still hear the door slam behind him and the chill as rain began to penetrate his clothes.

"You were sixteen?" she asked in an appalled voice. "What did you do? Where did you go? Your mother?"

"She was in South America, losing her battle with breast cancer." Not that she'd told her sons of her ill health. "We rarely saw her. Fernando was away with friends. The staff was forbidden to open a door to me. I didn't have shoes or a phone. I started walking and, honestly, the farther I got from him, the better I felt."

"Where did you sleep? How did you survive?"

He almost smiled at how maternal she already sounded.

"Someone picked me up, took me to a shelter for teens. A few weeks later, Fernando brought me some things—

my clothes and my ID. He gave me money. By then, I had a job selling souvenirs from a kiosk at festivals and cleaning up the site after the concerts were over. I was living in a house with ten other people, all of us down on our luck. Half of them were doing hard drugs. Others were hiding from immigration authorities or the law. The place was full of mold and infested with fleas, but I was so damned happy."

"Joaquin."

"Don't pity me," he said sharply. "It was the most agency I'd ever had. The most peace. I already knew what hell looked like. That was merely inconvenience."

"You didn't go to the police?"

"And say what? We'd had an argument and he told Fernando that I ran away. What if they sent me back to him?"

"Was Fernando safe with him?"

"He was old enough that Lorenzo thought twice about raising his hand to him."

"Is that why you were estranged from Fernando? Because he stayed with your father?"

"I don't blame him for that." He blamed himself for failing to spend more time with his brother when he had the chance. "I wanted him to join me on the outside, but he had put in the time and suffered in his own way. He felt he had earned his place at LVG."

"Even though it cost him *you*?" she choked.

"In his mind, he was claiming it for both of us. When Lorenzo had his heart attack, Fernando took charge and asked me to come aboard there. I was firmly estranged from Lorenzo by then. I didn't want anything of his. I was in Barcelona, scraping up financing for that gaming headset I told you about. Fernando persuaded Zurina's father to invest in me, giving me my start."

"That's another reason you left at the drop of a hat to help her," Siobhan said in a tone of hollow discovery.

"*Sí*. I would have kept my father out of my life forever, but when Fernando died, I had to come back into all of this." He waved abstractedly. "Fernando put up with his abuse for a legacy that means nothing, then died because he thought he could change out an electrical switch in a barn that should have been burned to the ground long ago. *Estúpida*!" He sliced his hand through the air. "But I won't let his suffering be in vain. He wanted his children to inherit LVG. So be it. I'll keep our father from destroying it with his pride and negligence. He's angrier than ever that I've usurped him, though. He'll come after me in whatever way he can. That's what my nightmare was about. He was coming for you."

"You think he'll be violent toward me?" She touched her chest, then her hand drifted lower, as though she wasn't aware of letting it settle on her abdomen. Her eyes widened in horror.

"I don't know." His stomach knotted. "But I can't afford to let down my guard. I *won't*. That's why I'm so adamant that you live with me."

She absorbed all of that with a frown of grave consternation.

"But I could..." Her brow flexed with anguish. "If you're that worried about my safety, I could stay with my sister after Christmas. And not tell anyone you're the baby's father."

Frost spread through his chest as he saw that, once again, his father was about to take something from him. Two people he wanted in his life very, very badly.

The harp strings of his phone's wake alarm began to play.

He hit Stop.

"I need to shower. My driver will be here soon."

Siobhan had wanted to know why he was so aloof. Now she did. Joaquin had been denied the security he was meant to feel within his family so he played his cards close to his chest. In fact, he'd been actively harmed by someone he ought to have been able to trust. Even his relatively good relationship with his brother had been twisted and cut short before it had had a chance to heal.

She couldn't be someone who hurt him, too. She couldn't isolate him from his baby, not when she knew what wellsprings of love they were. She had to give him an opportunity to be a father. For his sake and their child's.

Even if it tipped her equilibrium toward falling for him.

She was trying to be so careful with her feelings! But they were sliding like quicksilver, leaking and seeping out of her toward him, refusing to be caught back.

What would happen when he realized that?

That's another reason I didn't fight her leaving. I didn't want to lead her on.

He came into the bedroom a few minutes later. He was in his trousers again, but his hair was damp and his chest gleaming. He picked up his shirt from the chair and shook it out.

"I *will* keep you safe, Siobhan. I swear it," he said in a voice so vehement, her pulse skipped hard in her veins. "I wasn't trying to frighten you. I only want you to recognize the danger is real. But this situation won't go on forever. I won't allow it to."

"I believe you." She took another pair of slacks from the wardrobe and folded them into her suitcase. "But if I learned nothing else from the Sauveterres, it's that you can't live your life in fear. Take sensible precautions and go about your business, which is what I'll do. I'll move in with you if it makes you feel better, but I intend to keep working. At LVG."

The tension eased from his expression as he smoothly buttoned his shirt. "Those are your terms?"

"Yes."

"Provided your doctor agrees, I accept. But I live in Barcelona," he reminded.

"I know. I'll talk to Oladele about working remotely." She took the small win and continued packing, but paused when her phone vibrated on the night table.

She turned it over to see Cinnia was calling. A pained noise escaped her.

"What's wrong?"

"Nothing," she said heavily. "Just my sister. She tried me twice yesterday and I ignored her because..." The pregnancy news had consumed her. "She wants my ETA, but..." She looked to the gifts he'd wrapped and stacked so neatly. "What do I do about Christmas?"

"Spend it with your family." His face smoothed into

those unreadable lines that she found so frustrating. "I know you'll be safe there. I plan to work anyway."

"But..." She couldn't leave the father of her baby alone on Christmas mere days after they learned she was pregnant. What if something happened and she went into hospital? She would want him with her.

If she was only going to visit Cinnia, she might have confided her happy news, but everyone would be there and it was too soon to tell the world. The magnitude of holding on to her secret while fighting her anxiety over the holiday began to balloon in her mind. Tears welled in her eyes.

"Would you come?" she asked over the insistent buzz of her phone. "If I ask her...?"

Cortisol poured through her bloodstream as she recalled what had happened the last time she brought someone home for Christmas. Why was this so messy and *hard*?

Joaquin wouldn't betray her the way Gilbert had. Would he?

"If you want me to be there, yes." His dark eyes were fathomless. Some emotion flickered across his expression too quickly for her to interpret it. Wariness? Something warmer?

Relief eased the pressure in her chest. She pressed the quivering sensation from her lips and answered the video call, propping the phone against the bottom of her lamp so she was in the frame and Joaquin remained off camera.

"Hi, what's up?" she asked.

"Ramon said he offered to fly you down with him

and you said no." Cinnia had her blond hair pulled back with a headband and was working moisturizer into her clean face. She was fourteen years older than Siobhan, but looked closer to thirty than forty. "Do *not* tell me you're backing out."

"No. Work's been busy. They can't spare me." That wasn't entirely true if she was taking a few days of medical leave, but Cinnia didn't need to know about that. "I was planning to take the train Saturday—"

Joaquin shook his head.

"Sunday?" she asked.

"Is someone there with you?" Her sister's tone grew pointed and she stared hard through the screen. "On a workday? This early in the morning?"

"I was about to tell you," Siobhan grumbled. "I'm seeing someone. Ramon didn't say anything?"

"Should he have? Is it serious? Do you want to bring him to Christmas?"

"Just like that?" Despite her history? "You don't even know who he is."

"Of course, I do." Cinnia began brushing out her hair. "Ramon told Henri he thought something was going on between you. Henri told me. Why do you think I'm calling? Henri said he doesn't see any issue in having Joaquin join us so why don't you put me on to him and I'll invite him."

With a roll of her eyes, Siobhan handed the phone to Joaquin.

CHAPTER TWELVE

Joaquin discovered the only reason he had tolerated going into LVG was the opportunity to see Siobhan. Now that she was taking the week off for doctor visits and rest, being here felt more oppressive than ever.

Sleeplessness had something to do with his poor mood. And worry. Morning sickness had arrived the day she moved in and was hitting her at all hours. She had tried to sleep in the guest room, but he'd persuaded her to sleep with him so he could help her in the night if she needed it, fetching ice water and ginger tea and wringing out damp facecloths.

He hated seeing her miserable, and lying beside her while she slept was a delightful form of torture. He listened to her breathe, not touching her, afraid to move lest he wake her. Feeling her so close couldn't help but turn his mind to intimate acts, but he savored that time, too, feeling like an anchor coming to rest on the sea floor. *I'm not alone anymore.*

At the same time, he ached. *Ached.*

Trying to distract himself by thinking of what sort of father he'd make wasn't effective. It was too puzzling. And big. He kept trying to imagine knowing what to do with a crying baby, what to say as the baby grew old enough to talk. He'd never even held his brother's children, certain he'd break them. How would he become what his own child needed him to be?

When he finally did drift off, dark scenes from his past arrived. They always had Siobhan in them. His father would turn on her and Joaquin would be paralyzed, held back from protecting her. It was suffocating. Blood chilling.

Thankfully, today was his last in his father's office until the New Year. He left midmorning to meet Siobhan at the clinic where she was having her first scan, to confirm her due date. She had lined up a specialist in Barcelona where they would station themselves through her pregnancy, but they both wanted the peace of mind that this initial scan would hopefully provide.

She was already in a gown on the table when he was shown into a dimly lit room.

"How are you?" He took the hand she reached out, noting the bandage inside her elbow where she'd had blood drawn.

"Feeling like a captured alien being dissected for science. Oh! The nurse said my prenatal vitamins could be making me sick and gave me a different brand to try."

"That's good."

"Ready?" The technician cautioned, "Don't worry if we can't hear the heartbeat yet. At this stage, the heart isn't fully formed, but… Ah." As she began the scan, she brought up a grainy image of a kidney bean. The image wobbled then steadied. Something flickered. "That's the cardiac pulse."

All the air rushed out of Joaquin's lungs.

Siobhan turned her head, mouth trembling with a smile of wonder.

Such want rose in him then, he could hardly withstand it. He wanted this. He wanted the baby and the woman. He wanted a future he could believe in.

It was terrifying to want this hard. Especially when the level of responsibility a child represented threatened to crush him. He had somehow convinced himself this was no different than his duty to look out for Zurina and Fernando's children, but no. This was *his* baby. Conceived with a woman who was taking up increasing space in his life. Not just physically, but in the way she occupied his thoughts and stoked his emotions and held a spark of himself inside her.

The idea of her carrying a new life was like trying to contemplate the breadth of the universe. He had to shut his thoughts down before his skull cracked. He had to lock the greedy, hungry, possessive groaning beast within him behind a wall of reserve.

He had to consciously loosen his grip on Siobhan's hand so he wouldn't crush her bones and watched as the technician finished taking various measurements, studying the woman's face to be sure there were no flickers of concern.

A short time later, Siobhan was dressed and sitting beside him, waiting for the doctor to return to the consultation room.

"Are you okay?" Siobhan asked him warily.

"Yes," he said with surprise. "Are you?"

"Yes. But you went so quiet."

Because he was astonished. The full magnitude of her pregnancy was hitting him.

"Until now, my thoughts have all been around you, how I can support and protect you. Now I'm realizing there will soon be another person in my life. I'm trying to imagine what sort of father I'll make. I know I won't be abusive," he hurried to say, needing her to know that.

"I know," she said swiftly. Earnestly. "I think you'll be a wonderful father."

He winced and shook his head.

"I don't know if I'll be generous enough with myself." He kept thinking about her reservations about sleeping with him. About her fears that he would disappoint her by inciting feelings he couldn't return. "I've taught myself not to want things, so losing them doesn't matter. That's why I don't attach to people. The way my mother left… She had to. I understand that, but she got sick before I was able to spend more time with her. I lost her twice. Then Fernando…" He swallowed the ache in his throat. "It's easier to hold everyone at a distance. You can't do that to a child, though. You have to be open. Loving. I don't know if I can be." That was what he had tried to tell her the other night when he'd told her about Esperanza. That deep inadequacy tortured him as he thought about becoming a father.

"Trying is the first step and I know you'll do that." She reached across to squeeze his hand. "You're already trying to be there for your brother's children, even though it's difficult. That counts."

"It's not enough. I know that." It was frustrating to

feel so locked up inside. Not just broken, but like a bone that had healed wrong and couldn't change.

"Joaquin. Please trust me when I say this..."

Dios, she had the ability to sound tender and sweet. Her expression softened and he felt those wrongly healed bones inside him shift anyway, trying to straighten.

"Because I have been around a lot of babies. They are medically designed to latch on to your heart and pull it from your chest." Her tone turned rueful, her smile playful. "The big eyes? The pure, unconditional love they drool all over you? You won't stand a chance."

He snorted.

"You're really selling it," he said drily, but found her words irrationally reassuring.

The door opened and Joaquin reflexively closed his hand tighter on hers, holding his breath until he saw the doctor's smile.

"Everything looks as it should," the doctor said. He reviewed Siobhan's bloodwork with her and promised to send the results to her new doctor in Barcelona.

"Do you have any questions? Partners usually want to know about lovemaking." He sent a wink in Joaquin's direction before saying to Siobhan, "Provided you feel up for it, you may continue with your normal activities."

CHAPTER THIRTEEN

JOAQUIN HAD GONE back to the office after her scan, dropping Siobhan at the spa so she could have her hair done for the LVG Christmas party tonight.

After an afternoon of pampering that included a nap on the massage table, she arrived home to find him asleep on the bed, ankles crossed, arms folded, still dressed in his shirt and trousers from the office.

She softened her step as she crossed to the closet, not wanting to wake him when neither of them had been sleeping well since she'd moved in, but he'd shown her such concern, she'd melted every time.

More tender feelings had accosted her today when he'd revealed so much of himself. He'd pulled *her* heart from her chest as she recognized how much loss he'd suffered and how very hard it was for him to open himself as a result. It made her want to show him it was safe to let down his guard.

Even though letting her own guard down meant risking her heart even further.

"Siobhan?" He cleared the gruffness from his voice.

"Yes. I'm here." She poked her head out of the closet.

"Blond." He turned his head on the pillow, mouth quirking in a hint of a smile.

"Yes." She pulled a kimono over the bra and underwear she'd just changed into and came out to do a small twirl, showing him the way her hair had been styled half-up, half-down. "When I made the appointment, I was planning to have my roots touched up, but now that I'm pregnant, I don't want the chemicals on my scalp. This was foils and won't be so obvious when the color grows out."

"It's pretty. You are."

"You haven't seen my dress yet."

"I'm enjoying the lack of one, if I'm honest." He tucked his arm beneath his head and let his gaze track to where her legs were revealed by her short robe.

They hadn't talked about sex since the night he'd slept at her flat. She'd been sick and he'd been very chivalrous. It was all very Victorian.

But the doctor's endorsement had been heavy on her mind all afternoon, intertwining with her desire to feel closer to him. She did feel a lot better today, having skipped the troublesome vitamin.

Very tentatively, she slid one lapel of the robe off her shoulder, revealing the strap of her cranberry-red bra. "Any chance you're feeling festive?"

"Are you?" He didn't move, but his voice deepened. A watchful tension came over him. "I thought you preferred we keep things platonic."

She had been sincere when she said she was afraid she would fall in love with him, but she was already halfway there. And how could she convince him it was safe to love if she wasn't willing to let it happen to her?

"I also said sex would probably happen if I moved in," she said wryly, drawing the robe back onto her shoulder. "But if you don't want to…"

"I do," he said firmly. "Badly. I think about it a lot. But once we're down that road, it will be hard to go back."

"I know." She moved a little closer to the edge of the bed. "But I keep thinking that we're living together and starting a family and presenting ourselves as a couple. Shouldn't we try to be one? I mean…" Her smile turned itself upside down. "Fate must be wondering how many more messages it has to send."

"If we do this, it's because we're making that choice. You know that, right?"

"Yes. Sound mind and body," she said with a small eye roll.

"And you want to make that choice?" He held out his hand.

Very much.

Her heart turned over as she walked closer to the bed, shedding the kimono as she went.

His breath hissed in and his laser-focused gaze practically seared her skin as he took in the underwear that formed a V across her hips.

"But can you make love to me without ruining my hair and makeup?" she challenged as he guided her to sling one leg over his hips. She pinched her elbows together, using her upper arms to mash her breasts together, leaning forward so he had a good view of them threatening to spill from the tops of her bra cups. "Because I paid a lot of money to look this good."

"Worth every centimos," he said in a thick voice. His hands bracketed her hips. He dragged his gaze up to hers. "*Mi cielo*, I am certain you are about to ruin me. I'm looking forward to it."

She smiled, wallowing in a sense of feminine power as she opened his shirt buttons, starting at his waist and working her way up. As she shifted, his erection pressed beneath her.

He pushed his hand between them, adjusting himself. His knuckles brushed her mound, intimate and sending a flare of heat through her abdomen.

"You think about it a lot, too, hmm?" His mouth curled with wicked triumph. "That day in my office?" He turned his hand to cup her there, flexing his grip while his other hand skimmed her thigh then pressed her tailbone, encouraging her to press deeper into his palm. "Have you been aching for this?"

"Yes." Shattering tingles washed through her. She bit her lip, whimpering. Pressing. Struggling to finish spreading his shirt when her spine was beginning to melt.

She flowed down onto him, seeking the warm brush of his skin against her own. A kiss.

"Careful." He pushed his head into the pillow and set his hand against her collarbone, holding her off from pressing her mouth to his. "I have orders not to smudge. Which is going to happen if you're wet…"

He caressed her nape beneath the fall of her hair while he ran his amused, nibbling lips into her throat, sending shivers down her front so her breasts grew full and heavy. His other hand was still cradling the heat at her core, holding her in a delicious trap of sensuality.

Everything in her tightened, seeking *more*. She wanted him to roll her beneath him, but this was a game for him now, seducing her by delicate degrees—a scrape of his teeth at the edge of her jaw, the shift of his strong thighs pushing her legs wider so she sat deeper on his palm. The slide of his finger beneath the placket of silk to search out slick, slippery flesh that welcomed his exploring touch.

She moaned. For a long few minutes it was just that, her braced on shaking arms, enjoying the nibble of his lips in her throat and the caress of his touch.

"Bring this up to me," he said in a rasp when she began to dance her hips.

"What?" She blinked at him, dazed with lust.

He caught the lace against her hip and tugged. "Hold on to the headboard. Let me taste you."

It was utter debauchery, but the glitter of carnality in his eyes matched the needy hunger that gripped her. She shifted, allowing him to guide her into position and brush the silk placket aside and lick into the heart of her.

A guttural groan of pure wantonness left her.

His wicked hands moved over her, brushing her thighs and cradling her buttocks, shaping her breasts and holding her hips to encourage her to rock and seek and take her pleasure to the fullest.

In a sudden rush, a wave lifted her and crested, throwing her into a glorious maelstrom of pleasure, one that had her crying out in abandon.

Then, as she was still trembling and tingling and trying to catch her breath, he slid from beneath her and rose behind her.

"Don't move." She heard his zip and the rustle of his clothes. "Stay right there," he growled. His hand joined hers on the headboard, pinning one in place.

The rough fabric of his trousers arrived between her thighs. The cool teeth of his fly scored the underside of her buttock and she felt the graze of his knuckle as he guided his swollen tip against the pulsing, exposed flesh between her thighs.

She arched in welcome, moving her knees, offering. Inviting.

"Hold still, *mi reina*. I don't want to move a hair out of place—" His voice was lost in a ragged groan as he filled her with one slow thrust.

A fresh moan of joy left her, one of pleasure and luxury and homecoming.

"Gently, now," he whispered, palm splaying on her stomach then sliding downward. "Hold tight. Stay still."

He moved with disciplined power. While one hand slipped her bra strap off her shoulder, and his mouth branded her skin, his other hand caressed the soaked flesh clinging to the pistoning thickness of his. Within moments, she was sobbing in renewed joy, close, so close to breaking again.

"Wait for me." He slowed his touch. His strokes. "Wait. I'll tell you when."

She clenched the headboard in her hands. Clenched her eyes tight and clenched on him as she arched, held on the pinnacle in the most exquisitely fiendish way.

"Please, Joaquin," she sobbed. "Please now."

"Now." He clasped her hips and drove deep, shouting in triumph behind her.

CHAPTER FOURTEEN

AFTER TWO WHIRLWIND PARTIES, one at LVG and another in Barcelona for ProFab, they flew to Marbella in the south of Spain.

Joaquin had been ridiculously proud to have been seen with Siobhan's fingers laced between his own. She was beautiful, charming and graceful on the dance floor, making such evenings far more pleasant than they'd been in the past. He had anticipated some side-eye over the fact he was dating his employee, but an HR memo had circulated, explaining they had had a "brief relationship prior to the takeover." It was enough that any gossip about them had fizzled quickly.

After a lazy morning, they ate lunch on his plane. He was still stoned from their lovemaking, but Siobhan was unexpectedly quiet in a way that struck him as tense, especially on the drive into the hills from the Marbella airport.

"Are you feeling off?" he asked with concern.

"No. The new vitamins seem to be sitting better." She looked up from fiddling with the bracelet he'd won for her at his company's silent auction. It was an artistic blend of mismatched gold and silver links that she had seemed to love, but she looked on the verge of tears. "I'm nervous about bringing you here."

"You think I'll betray you or your family?" He captured her hand to still it, but was deeply unsettled. "You don't trust me?"

"No, I do." Her smile didn't stick, though. "I'm being silly."

He didn't get a chance to delve deeper. They stopped at a gate that read, *Sus Brazos*. Their driver greeted the guard who angled to send a smile at Siobhan.

"Welcome home, señora."

"Thank you, Baron." She found a smile for him. "Joaquin is my guest. He should be on the list."

"He is." The guard glanced between a screen and Joaquin, ensuring his identity, then waved them through.

"Do you mind taking the lower drive?" Siobhan asked the driver, who turned in to a winding lane that took them through olive and orange groves. They circled a pond and some gardens. She pointed through an orchard and down paths. "Stables. Staff housing. That's just a garden shed. There's a playhouse for the children. You can't see the tennis courts, but they're behind those trees."

Joaquin would have thought she was eagerly showing off the place she considered home if her nails hadn't been digging into the back of his hand. She was putting off their arrival as long as possible.

"Siobhan." He gently squashed her hand. "It will be okay. Nothing bad will happen."

Her lip briefly quivered and he read the message in her eyes. *You don't know that.*

They arrived in a cobbled courtyard with a fountain.

Wide steps led up to a pair of huge doors on a Spanish colonial mansion.

Cinnia trotted out with a handful of staff behind her.

She was even more like Siobhan in person. They had similar figures, both slender yet curvy. They were the same height, had the same profile and sounded the same as they greeted each other with equally effusive hugs.

"You've made me so happy!" Cinnia declared, pressing her baby sister back to blink her wet lashes at her. "And you've gone back to blond. *Much* better, but I may be biased." She flicked at her bobbed hair, then hugged Joaquin. "Thank you for bringing her. You have singlehandedly saved Christmas."

"My work here is done, then," he drawled, thinking for Cinnia, perhaps, but what about for Siobhan?

They entered an empty foyer with a curved staircase that swept up to a gallery. A huge, unlit crystal chandelier hung in the dome of colored glass that poured stains of red and purple and green onto the marble floor.

"Where is everyone?" Siobhan asked.

"Tennis tourney. I said I'd bring you down once you arrived, but the nannies have the children in the movie room, waiting for you."

A gasp from the top of the stairs lifted all their eyes.

"You're here!" The voice of wonder belonged to a girl of ten or so. She gripped the rail and beamed with joy over it. She turned her head and started to yell, "She's he—"

"Wait!" Siobhan hurried up the stairs. "Hugs first. Come here."

The girl hurried to meet her on the stairs and they

hugged tight. Siobhan kissed her a dozen times all over her face, making the girl giggle, then Siobhan pointed down at Joaquin.

"Look. I brought someone and I don't want to scare him. Your special job is to gather all the children and tell them to queue oldest to youngest. Bring them here so I can introduce them and we can all get our hugs. Can you do that for me?" She kept herself at eye level and tucked the girl's hair behind her ear.

"I'll tell Lettie to do it. She's the bossiest." The girl spun to race away.

"That's the real reason Cin begged me to come," Siobhan said as she came back to the bottom of the stairs. She flicked a teasing look at her sister. "I'm the only one who can literally keep these pelicans in a line."

"True story," Cinnia confided to Joaquin. "Bear with us. They're very excited. Once we get this greeting out of the way, you can take cover in your room. Oh. Here we go."

Giggles and stifled squeals accompanied the shuffle of footsteps as children appeared on the landing, dutifully walking in a line. They wore a range of outfits from jeans and pullovers to frilly dresses to a superhero costume and a pair of pajamas. They broke into big smiles and waved energetically through the rail when they saw her, but the girl at the front sent a stern look that kept them from breaking rank.

"Look at you all so well behaved. Thank you," Siobhan said. "Lead them down here, Lettie."

The girl who had hugged Siobhan on the stairs came

to the bottom step, so she was standing right in front of Siobhan.

No. That wasn't the same girl. Twins, Joaquin recalled as he looked between her and the girl behind her. Identical blue eyes blinked at him with curiosity. In fact, as he looked up the stairs, he saw more twins.

"Señor Joaquin Valezquez is my guest. You may call him Tío Joaquin. And he prefers Spanish?" she asked.

"French and English work, too."

"Good. Okay. Pay attention," she warned him over her shoulder. "There will be a quiz later." Siobhan set her hands on the first girl's shoulders. "This is Colette, Cinnia and Henri's daughter and Rosie's twin."

Rosie leaned out to wave at him. "You can tell us apart because I like to wear pink and Lettie only sometimes does."

Lettie did not introduce herself as the bossy one, but she did stick out her hand in a way that reminded him of her father and uncle. Very sure of herself. "It's nice to meet you."

"The pleasure is mine," Joaquin said sincerely as he shook her hand.

"Very nice." Siobhan hugged Colette and kissed her cheek, earning a wrinkled nose and a happy smile before Colette moved to the other side of the stairs and sat down.

Rosie led everyone down a step. "Are you Auntie Dorry's boyfriend?" she asked.

"I am," Joaquin said.

"Hmm." Her little brows went up in speculation as she moved to sit behind her sister.

A boy came next, tall with dirty blond hair and ice-blue eyes.

"Prince Tyrol of Elazar," Siobhan said. "King Xavier and Queen Trella's eldest."

Right. They were spending Christmas with royalty. Two pair of monarchs, in fact.

Siobhan hugged Tyrol with all the enthusiasm and familiarity she had shown her sister's children, kissing his cheeks until he chuckled and pushed her away.

"Please call me Tyrol," the boy said when Siobhan released him to shake Joaquin's hand. "We don't use titles when we're with family."

"Tyrol is only a few weeks younger than the girls," Siobhan said. "This is Malik, Prince of Zhamair. His parents are King Kasim and Queen Angelique." Siobhan warmly embraced the boy who came next. "Play chess against him if you like to lose."

He flashed a grin. He was perhaps a year younger than the other children with light brown skin and black hair. His intense brown eyes were surrounded by the sort of thick eyelashes women coveted.

The next boy led the group down another step.

"This reminds me of that old movie where the children sing on the stairs at their parents' party," Joaquin said with a smirk.

Rosie gasped. "*We* should do that."

Siobhan touched her lips, urging her to silence as she introduced, "Miguel, Ramon and Izzy's eldest."

Did her voice shake a tiny bit? Did she hug this boy a little longer and harder and look a little more distressed as she did it?

Her love for all of these children was very obvious in how well she knew each of them and how much affection they were showing her. It drove home for Joaquin how truly devastated she must have been to have caused any sort of peril for them. He instantly wanted to find this man who had broken her faith in herself and find a way to make him sorry.

She released Miguel and greeted the next boy with an affectionate smooth of his sandy blond hair. "Remy is Henri and Cinnia's son. He's turning seven on my birthday."

"We're birthday twins," he said and moved to sit with the others.

"Do us together. *Please*, Auntie Dorry?" A girl of about five stepped down so she was on the same step as the one ahead of her. The pair of girls had strikingly similar features, but distinctly different hair and skin colors.

"This is Genevieve, Princess of Zhamair." Siobhan bent to squash the girls together, making them giggle before she released them to cup the other girl's beaming face. "And Vivien, Princess of Elazar. Our cousin-twins."

"Oh? Same birthday?"

"Uh-uh. My mama couldn't hold me in her womb so Tía Gili did it," Vivien explained. "We have different mommies and daddies so we're cousins, but we're still twins because we grew together and were born together."

Joaquin was impressed by the science, the startlingly selfless act by one sister for another, and the fact these girls had a grasp on what made them unique.

"Finally, Maya and Sofia, Ramon and Izzy's twins." Siobhan stretched her arms to hug the last pair together, too, eyes sheening with fresh tears before she closed them. "Maya and Sofia are five, same as the cousin-twins."

"We thought they were the last batch in the oven, then we got the big news," Cinnia said.

Joaquin snapped a look to Siobhan. Had she told her sister?

"That's right. Two are missing!" Siobhan tucked her fists on her hips and pretended to search around her feet. "Lettie?"

"I tried to take them yesterday, to play house," Colette said. "Mama said no."

"Aren't you the killjoy," Siobhan teased Cinnia.

"I know, right?"

"We'll meet Gili and Kasim's twins later. Thank you for using your best manners." Siobhan clapped her hands. "Go back to what you were doing. We'll play hide-and-seek after dinner if you want to."

"Yes!" The children raced up the stairs.

Siobhan kept a smile on her face as they left, but it hardened and cracked when Cinnia wrapped her arm around her waist.

"See? They just wanted you here. We all do. You're shaking." Cinnia drew back to look at her, gaze widening in alarm.

"I'm fine." Siobhan brushed her off.

Joaquin saw how pale she was and clasped her cold hand.

"We had a late night at my company Christmas party," he lied. They'd actually left early, but Cinnia didn't need to know that. "Do you mind if we freshen up before we meet everyone else?"

* * *

Siobhan thought she was doing a credible job of keeping her emotions in check. She wasn't even sure why she was having such a rattled reaction. The children were all safe and healthy and happy. Their hugs always filled up spaces inside her that she wasn't aware had run empty.

But the whole time she'd been greeting them, she'd been suffering a growing sense of doom. Of failure. Guilt.

She brought Joaquin into the mini-suite that had been hers since moving here ten years ago. Cinnia had had it freshened up when Siobhan had left for London to live with Ramon and Izzy, so it was now a more neutral green instead of mauve. The hard-used computer desk and worn-in love seat had been replaced with sleek, comfortable new ones. The top quilt on the bed was no longer printed with periodic symbols. The bedding had been converted to the standard Sauveterre issue of blue with a yellow stripe.

It was still "Dorry's room," though. The shelves around the parlor area were stuffed with her old textbooks. The photo of herself with glasses, braces and a big smile, holding the newborn Rosie and Lettie, was still on the night table. The bathroom and walk-in closet were stocked with a selection of her favorite cosmetics and clothes.

Joaquin's things were already hanging in there, she noticed with a small double-take. That was weird, but nice.

"If you need anything, the house phone connects to the kitchen." She pointed to the cordless extension on the desk. "They relay messages to the drivers or security or whoever you're looking for. The doors to the balcony stick in winter. I'll show you how to do it." She swept the drapes away from the glass and unlatched the lock.

"Siobhan." Joaquin turned her and wrapped his arms around her in a hug that was tight enough to immobilize her. He ran his hands over her, smoothing all the fraying threads coming off her. "Catch your breath."

A tiny sob escaped her. She clutched at him. How had he known?

"I don't know why I'm upset," she said in frustration. "I love them so much and I want to be here, but…"

He didn't say anything, only closed his arms tighter around her, tucking her head into the hollow of his shoulder as though sheltering her from danger.

"You're right," she admitted in a strained voice as angry heat rose behind her breastbone. "I hate her."

"Who?" He lifted his head to look down on her, gaze sparking with battle readiness.

"Dorry." The scalding sensation traveled from behind her heart up to her throat. "I don't want to be her. She's thoughtless and naive and stupid. She doesn't deserve to be loved by all of those children who trust her. But I have to be her to be *here*." She brushed at a tickle on her cheek and realized it was a tear. "God, I'm pathetic."

She tried to turn away, but he kept her in the cage of his arms, holding her before him, unable to hide from herself or him.

"Why can't you forgive yourself and let it go?" he asked.

"Because they're innocent children!" She flicked her

fingers toward the door. "I walked a wolf right into their home."

"Did you sneak him in? I thought you said Ramon allowed you to bring him into their home."

"Yes, but they all spoil me." She'd been a child herself when she came here. Henri and his family had indulged her at every turn. "Ramon trusted me to have a gauge on someone I was *sleeping* with. Someone I claimed to love."

He flinched, but only said, "You didn't *let* him betray you, Siobhan. He just did it." There was a ragged edge in his voice that told her he understood that type of pain at a soul-deep level. "Is it really Dorry you hate? Or how badly she got hurt? Is turning your back on her your way of hiding from *that*?"

A pulse of anguished discovery shot through her. It was the jump-scare of catching her own reflection in a mirror. More of those stupid, stupid tears rose in her eyes because one word was lighting up her brain. *Yes*.

She was deeply hurt and deeply angry that she'd been hurt. Her life had been one where she had been smothered in love. She had opened her heart to Gilbert as innocently as those children opened theirs to her. Having her heart stomped on and tossed away had been shocking. Unbearable.

"You're not the villain here." His graveled voice stirred her hair.

"I know, but..." She had to bite her lips to keep them from trembling. Her chest felt full of pins. "How could I love someone so awful? I feel foolish. I thought we were going to get married and... I keep thinking that I let it happen because I was in a hurry for this." She drew back to wave a hand at the room around them. The house and the family within it.

She began to shake again because she was laying bare more than her hurt and her heart. She was telling him what she wanted from *him*. And she already knew he might not be able to give it to her.

"I want a partner in life. I want children. Not just this baby." She touched her abdomen. "But siblings. A family. I want big gatherings and silly arguments over holidays and all the love—"

This wasn't supposed to be a test, but she sensed the way he withdrew a little, hiding his thoughts while she cleared her throat and continued to speak.

"—that I see when everyone is together like this. I always envied Cin for having this when I lived here. That's what I feel like I don't deserve after bringing Gilbert into their lives. I thought he was going to give me this and he *didn't*." The scored sensation behind her sternum deepened. "He showed me why I couldn't have it."

"Do you still love him?" Tension entered his body, as though bracing for a blow.

"No." The irony was she had hated Gilbert for so long, she couldn't remember why she had thought she loved him. He'd been a master at witty observations and charming compliments. He had claimed to want what she wanted—travel and a concentration on career, then a family. It had all been a lie, though. He hadn't even been good in bed! Not like…

Don't. The fact that Joaquin gave her orgasms didn't mean she ought to fall for him. *Don't fall in love again*, she warned herself, but the layers of her defenses were peeling away like broken eggshells. Joaquin wasn't even trying to get under her skin! He was only being himself: honest and honorable and protective. Holding her when she was upset. He didn't see through her. He *saw* her.

It was deeply perturbing, not because she didn't feel safe with him, but because she did. What if she was setting herself up for another grave disappointment?

The more time she spent with him, however, the more her turmoiled emotions around Gilbert became flaky remnants she was happy to discard. Letting go of her hurt and anger and guilt made room for this: for Joaquin and the things she felt for him that were already far stronger and sweeter and hotter and more enduring than she'd felt for anyone else ever.

She was falling in love with him, she realized with a lurch in her heart. And she wanted him to love her back.

Was it even possible for him to love, though? Was it possible for him to love *her*?

The yearning in her was so strong, she could only stare at the tab on his quarter-zip pullover, trying to hold back the burst of emotion that was threatening to crest again and spill over in fresh tears.

"You were young, Siobhan. You made a mistake. We all do that." He smoothed her hair and pressed it against her skin as he tucked his hand against her neck. "But the way you're punishing yourself puts me in an impossible position."

She frowned up at him. "How?"

"I won't tolerate anyone being cruel to the mother of my child." His thumb caressed the edge of her jaw. "So

I must insist you set your anger aside, *cariño*. Be kind to yourself."

"Or you'll do what?" she asked on a chuckle of reluctant humor.

"Distract you. Coax you into a better mood." He dipped his head to graze a light kiss against her lips. "Remind you that you deserve to be treated well."

A spark of sensuality flew directly into her center and began to burn. He *was* distracting her. He was making her feel cosseted and appreciated and understood. He was making her feel *hope*.

And maybe, just maybe, she was lucky that Gilbert had disappointed her so badly. Otherwise, she wouldn't be here in this moment with this man. Maybe fate really had had a plan.

That thought was a jostling turn of a kaleidoscope, rearranging all her dark, jagged thoughts into new, colorful patterns. Something that dazzled.

"How well?" she asked as she stole her fingers into his hair. "Teach me a lesson."

"That would be my pleasure." He claimed her mouth with his own and reached past her to yank the curtain back into place.

CHAPTER FIFTEEN

I WANT THIS, Siobhan had said of the big family and the endearing chaos they created.

As the day wore on, Joaquin began to see the appeal. There was a lot of laughter and teasing and children scooped up by loving arms that belonged to the nearest adult.

He also caught a glimpse of the indulgent mother Siobhan would become. It did something to his heart when he saw her with the youngest princes of Zhamair, cooing and cradling the identical twins. It caused a stretching sensation in his chest that stole his breath.

The princes were five months, he was told. Both were strong, determined little wrestlers. They smiled at her, chewed their fists, batted clumsily at each other, then dug their toes into her while trying to scale her shoulders.

"Do you need me to hold one of them?" Joaquin was compelled to ask, experiencing the strangest impatience to see her cradle their own baby. To hold it himself.

"Don't you dare." She expertly firmed her arms around them. "The only thing better than holding one baby is holding two."

"Auntie Dorry is our baby whisperer," their father,

Kasim, told him. "That's why Gili and I had twins. I was assured Dorry could be persuaded to come live with us."

"Oy, you did this on purpose, did you?" she teased. "Well, I'm tempted." She dipped her chin to nuzzle one round cheek, expression tender. "Maybe I'll take them home with me. You wouldn't mind, would you?"

"I think you're finally old enough for me to say this to you, little one, but *make your own*." Kasim stole one of his sons and held him over his head, pretending to eat the boy's guts and making the boy giggle.

Siobhan sent Joaquin a look of amusement at their shared secret. Job done.

An electric sensation struck Joaquin. It was a primal desire that went far beyond sexual want. Beyond his desire for her and their baby to be safe and comfortable. Beyond anything he had ever wanted for himself. He wanted this for *her*.

Which made it imperative to remove any threat from his father, once and for all.

He brought that up when he finished battling Henri on the tennis court the following morning.

Joaquin had won, but not easily. They sat down to orange juice and toasted bread smeared with olive oil, crushed tomatoes and slices of dry-cured jamón, watching Ramon and Isabella play Trella and Xavier.

"I presume Ramon relayed everything I told him in Madrid about my conflict with my father over LVG?" Joaquin asked.

"He did." Henri brushed his fingers on his napkin.

"I'm taking off the gloves with him. There could be

blowback against Siobhan. And your family, once her connection to you is known."

"Then stop seeing her," Henri said.

I can't, Joaquin almost said, thinking of the baby, but that was Siobhan's news to share when she was ready and the truth was, "I don't want to."

"This is serious, then?" Henri pressed. "You're in love with her?"

With Henri's astute gaze pinned on him, Joaquin felt as though he had his neck fully exposed, but he hated to show his hand—or his heart. Especially when he was so unsure of his ability to give it.

"My intentions are honorable, yes." He wanted to spend his life with her. He had known that from the moment he'd seen the pulse of their baby's heartbeat on the screen. No, the glimmer of a future with her had first flickered to life within him when she'd asked, *What will we do if...* Before that, even, when he had wished for more time than a single night in San Francisco.

"Having said that," Joaquin continued gravely, "I'd like to prevail on you for a favor, in the interest of time. I know how this request looks, or would in Siobhan's eyes. Hear me out."

Henri nodded curtly.

"I'm working at buying up my father's debts. Some of his creditors feel enough loyalty to him that they're refusing to sell to me, but if you were to approach them through your channels, he wouldn't know I was pulling the strings. I'm not asking you to be out of pocket. I'll cover everything."

Henri waved off that detail, even though they both knew they were talking eight and nine figures.

"It's a delicate situation. I need to keep Siobhan's true identity off my father's radar until I've crippled him. Otherwise, he has a fresh and effective avenue to attack me."

"Us," Henri said with a grimace.

"Exactly. I would call him ruthless, but *reckless* is the better word. This favor isn't without risk for you. Say the word and I'll look at other options."

"The day he comes for my family is the day *I* cripple him," Henri said. "Does she need extra security?"

"I'm arranging that."

Henri nodded thoughtfully. "Have you discussed this with her?"

"Not yet." Joaquin grimaced again. "She would be devastated if she thought she was the reason my father came after any of you. I don't even want to put the potential of it into her head."

"Don't. She puts too much pressure on herself for our safety. That's my job, not hers. And she can't hide her connection to us forever. It sounds as though your father will become a problem to me eventually. I'm making the decision to deal with it now, while it's easily contained. Do you have a list of targets and timelines?"

"I do."

Christmas Day was utter perfection, filled with food and torn paper and nonstop laughter—especially when Malik discovered that all the gifts Joaquin had wrapped were missing name tags.

She and Joaquin looked at each other, perplexed.

"You said you'd do it," he reminded her.

"I did!" She burst out laughing.

Everyone groaned, but she recovered by having each child find a gift that was missing a tag. It turned into a game to open it and give it to whoever was the intended recipient. The children loved it.

Her gift for Joaquin *was* labeled. He looked uncomfortable accepting it, saying, "You didn't have to get me anything."

"I wanted to," she insisted and had to wonder whether he was given gifts very often. By his reaction, she suspected not.

He frowned with curiosity as he unwrapped the framed photo. He read the accompanying certificate. "You bought me a race car?"

"A share in the team Ramon is buying. You seemed interested when I mentioned it last week."

"I can honestly say this is something I didn't know I wanted, but I'm delighted to have. Thank you." He kissed her then dropped a gift in her lap that contained a pair of earrings he "thought would suit her."

The large, pear-shaped aquamarines were suspended from a shimmering row of brilliant-cut diamonds. When she joined him in bed that evening, she wore only them and thanked him by kissing her way down his torso, eventually making her way back to his lips.

"Not just for the jewelry," she whispered when his heart was still pounding and all the tension had left his body. "Thank you for being here with me. You helped me remember why I love this time of year."

She was in love with him, she realized in a rush of

clarity. It was a wide, glorious light inside her, one that felt so distinctly *right* she didn't know why she'd fought it. Joaquin might still be reticent at times, but he was a fiercely protective, caring, indulgent man.

Her love was so fresh and new and perfect, she almost said it aloud.

But he was twisting to roll her beneath him, kissing her with ravenous passion.

"My turn to have a peek under the tree. I think there's one more gift for me." He parted her legs and slid down.

CHAPTER SIXTEEN

THEY LEFT THE next day, amid pleas to stay longer. Ramon and Izzy were staying through the end of the year, but both royal families were needed at home.

"Joaquin has work and we're attending a New Year's Eve gala. But I'm not so far away anymore," Siobhan reminded Cinnia. "Come see us anytime."

They hugged it out and Siobhan was still floating in warm, happy vibes when they arrived back in Barcelona.

She *loved* his home here. It was two stories in an older building and managed to be both spacious and cozy at the same time. There was a comfortable breakfast nook in a sunny corner of the kitchen and a wraparound terrace that looked onto the sea. A Jacuzzi tub stood on the balcony off the primary suite surrounded by wintering shrubs strung with fairy lights. Empty flowerboxes promised a riot of color in the spring.

After all the drama at LVG and the shock of her pregnancy and the busy-ness that had led up to Christmas, she needed the pleasant bubble of contentment that encased them between Christmas and New Year's. Joaquin mostly worked from home while she read a book on pregnancy and combed through a contract for him, making notes that had him saying, "Good catch." They cuddled in the evening while watching movies, slept late and made love midday because *why not*?

It was a life she could get used to. It was the life she wanted. With him.

But it only lasted until the last day of the year.

Neither of them had left the penthouse much and, now that they were away from Madrid and LVG, Siobhan had begun to believe Lorenzo no longer posed a threat. It was the sort of complacency she should have known better than to fall into, but she did.

She booked herself into a spa for the day, one where she knew the massage would put her to sleep. She needed a nap if she was going to stay awake until midnight tonight.

Toward the end of her pampering, when her makeup was done and the stylist was finishing her hair for the party, the woman in the chair next to her looked up from her phone.

"Are you Dorry Whitley?"

The bottom fell out of her stomach. Siobhan reached for her phone while playing it off with a confused, "Why do you ask?"

"This is you, isn't it?" The woman angled her screen to show Siobhan her own face.

Her phone rang in her hand. It was Joaquin.

"Are you safe?" he asked tightly.

"I think so." Ripples were traveling through the salon. She was getting surreptitious looks. "Qahira is here." As a precaution, Joaquin had hired her a bodyguard, one who had so far had precious little to do since she left the house so rarely. "What happened?"

"My father must have discovered your identity. The gossip sites are showing photos of us in Madrid with headlines about Dorry Whitley surfacing after being missing for years."

As though she was some sort of criminal who'd gone into hiding and had suddenly been spotted? Yuck. But it didn't surprise her. It was exactly the type of made-up scandal the press had pinned on the Sauveterres for years.

"I'll call Cin and warn her."

"Stay there. I'm coming to get you."

"No, I'm almost done. I'll leave in a moment." She glanced at the woman doing her hair. The woman nodded.

In the few minutes it took for her to put on her coat, someone from inside the spa had sold the tip. A number of photographers were gathered outside the spa in the courtyard entrance of potted trees that surrounded a reflecting pool.

Siobhan's driver pulled the SUV up as closely as he could, but there was no straight path to it. She had to walk around the water into one of the lines of photographers.

As she stepped outside with Qahira, the piranhas closed in, snapping their cameras. That caught the attention of several passersby who halted to record her with their phones. Someone shoved a microphone toward her face and asked a question in Spanish.

Qahira blocked him and shouted for everyone to "Move back!"

Siobhan saw an opening and tried to dart through, but was yanked to a stop when someone grabbed her arm.

She reacted on instinct, surprising her attacker by flowing into the force of his tug on her arm. She continued into a pivot, pulling the photographer off balance. As she did that, she ducked low and threw her hip into his groin. She heard his breath leave him as she reached behind her shoulder, grabbed behind his neck, got her back into his stomach and used his own momentum and the strength in her thighs to lift him off his feet.

She flipped him into the pool of water. His camera clattered to the bricks and the splatter of drops hitting the pavement was overloud. Everyone froze in shock.

"That's what you get when you touch someone without their permission," Siobhan said. "Who's next?" She took a threatening stomp toward the nearest person holding a cell phone.

Everyone stumbled backward.

"Señora." Qahira opened her long arms, forming a barrier while the driver opened the back door of the SUV.

Siobhan dove in.

Joaquin was livid when he saw the footage. *Livid*.

Siobhan's altercation with the photographer was posting on all the social media channels and entertainment sites, all from different angles, all showing her defending herself from the attack.

She called him from the car to reassure him she was safe. Then Killian called him as Joaquin was watching it. Then Henri called him. Siobhan's phone was pinging like popcorn as he met her in the lobby of his building.

"I'm taking you to the hospital," he said as he tried to keep himself from crushing her in his twitching, battle-ready arms.

"I'm fine," she insisted. "Shaken up, but that photographer will be the one wearing bruises." She pulled away and stalked into the elevator.

Joaquin waited until they were in the apartment to say, "The baby?"

"Fine, I think." Her profile turned stiff and wan. "I wasn't hurt and I was moving furniture before I knew I was pregnant. Nothing happened. I'll see a doctor if it becomes necessary, but for now, I'd rather be here where I'm safe and comfortable."

If it became necessary. The mere thought of her losing the baby made him sick. If she went through anything more because of his father—

Joaquin closed his eyes. He couldn't let himself think of it. It made him too murderous. This had to end. *Today*.

"No, you don't have to come," Siobhan was telling her mother over video chat. "I promise I'm fine. This will blow over in a few days— Yes, I know, but now that I know I'm doxxed, I'll take precautions. Yes. Cup of tea. Feet up. I'm doing it now. Tell the girls I'm fine, but I'm turning off my phone for a while. Thank you. I love you, too." She sank onto the sofa and blew out a long breath.

"Will you put the kettle on for me?" Siobhan called while she watched the video. "Oh, come on," she couldn't help exclaiming.

"What?" Joaquin asked shortly. "I thought you were turning that off."

"I was on the phone the whole way here. I hadn't seen the video." She sent him a bright grin, then looked back at the screen. "Whenever I took those self-defense classes, they would warn me that it's different in real life, that I might freeze in shock, but muscle memory works. I look like a freaking action star. And could I have been more camera ready?" She pointed at the hair and makeup that had withstood her tussle and was still on point and tapped Watch Again. "I'm so glad I wore those boots today."

"It's not funny, Siobhan," he near shouted.

"It kind of is." She couldn't help her smirk. "The guy looks like a cat that fell in the toilet."

"Nothing about this is funny."

She sobered as she took in his hair standing in spikes from his agitated fingers, his grim expression and the light of torment in his eyes.

"You're right. I'm sorry." She dropped her phone onto the cushions and rose to hug his waist, finding his body had turned to concrete, but his arms locked tightly around her. "I'm sorry you were worried about me." She rubbed her cheek on his chest then tilted her head back. "But don't you find it a little bit reassuring that I can take care of myself?"

"You shouldn't have to!" He pulled away and shot his hand into his hair again.

"I know, but this isn't your fault. We don't even know if your father is behind it. Someone else may have recognized me."

"No, it was my father," he said grimly, pacing a few steps. "Henri called me just before you arrived. I've been using him as a go-between to buy up some of Lorenzo's debts. One of the creditors put it together and tipped off my father to my plan."

"Wait, what? You were using Henri?" Her heart juddered to a stop in her chest. Her whole body went cold.

Joaquin held up a hand. "That was a poor choice of word. I asked Henri at Christmas to let me use his channels, so my father wouldn't know I was behind the buying of his debts. We were trying to stay ahead of my father learning of your connection to the Sauveterres. I knew he would exploit it once he found out."

"Why didn't you tell me?" She waved an agitated hand.

"I didn't want to upset you."

"And you knew I would be upset," she said, growing worse than upset. "You knew this was a red line for me. I thought you wanted *me*. Not Henri and his resources. I thought you and I were growing closer. I thought I could trust you." She had fallen in *love* with him.

"You can," he swore, but the shadows of betrayal stayed heavy over her heart.

She shook her head, wondering how she could have been so stupid. Again.

"For God's sake, Siobhan. This is what he does." Joaquin's voice shook. "If he can't take what I have, he destroys it. Don't let him do that to *us*."

"What *us*? I'm here because I thought we were a team. A partnership." She had to blink fast because her eyes were welling. "I trusted you so *you* would trust *me*. I took a chance for our baby. For *you*. I wanted to show you it was safe to love me so I—" Her throat flexed, nearly closing over the words. "I let myself fall in love with you."

He drew a rough breath and held out a hand, but she brushed it away.

"Don't act like that's news to you. I told you it could happen! I thought at the very least it was *safe* to love you, but it's not."

A number of emotions flashed across his face before he shuttered his expression, brick by brick.

"It's not safe, no," he said in a tone that was so grim, it lifted the hairs on the back of her neck. "Not until I've dealt with him once and for all." He picked up his phone and walked to the door.

Her blood was congealing in her veins at how murderous he sounded. "What are you going to do?"

"Whatever I have to."

"Joaquin, stop," she cried, truly afraid he would do something he couldn't undo. "How does leaving like this reassure me you're in this relationship for *me*? I need to feel like I'm more than a means to an end, but you're choosing hating him over loving me. Do you see that? He is not the one tearing us apart. *You* are."

"What do you want me to do?" His voice was tortured. "Tell you I love you and beg you to stay here until I get back?" He shook his head in a way that negated his thrown-away words. "You're better off as far away from me as you can get."

Her brittle heart cracked. "Then I won't be here when you get back," she warned.

His breath cut in as though her words had been a knife

into his chest, but he only asked, "Where will you go? Your sister's?"

"What do you care where I go?"

He didn't even say, *I care*. He just left.

CHAPTER SEVENTEEN

SIOBHAN DIDN'T LET herself agonize over whether to leave. She knew she would always have doubts about Joaquin and his motives if she stayed.

So she left.

The safest thing would have been to go south, back to her sister's, but she didn't want to pretend for the children and everyone else that she was fine. She wasn't fine. She was devastated. Brokenhearted.

She wanted to be alone. She felt foolish, exactly as she had after she had trusted Gilbert, so she went north. Home. To her mother's empty house in London. Where she had gone the last time.

Her eyes stung the whole way, but she fought back the tears. She could accept that Joaquin wanted to vanquish his father, but why hadn't he told her what he planned? She felt used again. Betrayed again.

And shut out. Why didn't he ask *her* to help? She was actually a very spicy bitch when crossed. Had he not seen how she had treated that man who had grabbed her?

That gauntlet of photographers had actually been really frightening. Once she was in the car, all she had wanted was to be home with Joaquin. Safe in his arms.

He *had* made her feel safe. Until this.

Four hours after hastily packing, she arrived in Hertfordshire.

The house she had grown up in was an older home on a property of mature trees and well-tended flowerbeds. It had been bordering on shabby when she'd been young. Their mother had barely been hanging on to it. They had all worked to keep things afloat. Cinnia had had her estate practice, the middle girls had worked in pubs and shops. Siobhan had shared a room with Cin so her mother could rent hers out. Aside from earning a few pounds babysitting, Siobhan had been too young to contribute, which had always made her feel like a liability.

Once Cinnia married Henri, everything changed, insisting the house receive a complete upgrade so it had top-notch security and a twelve-foot wall around the garden.

As she entered the code for the door, and Qahira moved into the shadows to ensure the house was empty, Siobhan thought of that old song that began, *Hello, darkness*. Except it wasn't her friend. It just made her feel melancholy.

"Clear," Qahira reported.

Siobhan thanked her and moved through the house, turning up the heat and putting on some lights.

The decor had also been refreshed in recent years. The floor was now a posh golden hardwood. There was a piano beneath the floating staircase, and the potting shed was a proper guest cottage where Qahira would stay.

Siobhan went upstairs to unpack, almost turning out of habit into the room she had once shared with Cinnia. Rather than two singles, it now held bunk beds for the twins to use when Cinnia visited their mother here.

That had Siobhan remembering Christmas and the fact Joaquin had attended the festivities with her. At the time, she had thought he had gone for *her*. Now she was questioning his motives. Had he been wanting to speak to Henri all along?

No. He could have talked to Ramon when Ramon was in Madrid. The fact was he didn't *need* her to use the Sauveterres. And Henri wasn't stupid. He wouldn't allow himself to be used. He would have had his own reasons for helping Joaquin.

Even if Joaquin had gone there specifically to ask Henri for a favor, he had still helped her work through her anger at herself. He had helped her build memories she would cherish for a lifetime. He had restored her joy in the holiday.

She closed her eyes against emotive tears as she remembered the way he had brushed off Maya's palm when she had stumbled.

"You need to kiss it," Maya had insisted. So he had.

He was going to be a magnificent father. She knew that deep in her bruised heart.

She believed he wanted to be a supportive husband, too. That was why he was trying to keep her safe. He did care about her. He had demonstrated that in countless ways, but she had let her insecurities get in the way. She had jumped straight to being used because it was easier to believe that was where her worth to him lay than that he valued *her*.

She was still devaluing *herself*. Acting as though she

was silly Dorry Whitley, whom people saw as a conduit to power and money, when Dorry Whitley was actually a powerful badass in her own right. Everyone online was saying so.

Joaquin had let her go, though. The same way he had let Esperanza go when her feelings grew deeper than he was comfortable accepting.

He didn't love her.

Or did he?

What do you want me to do? Tell you I love you and beg you to stay here until I get back. You're better off as far away from me as you can get.

Had he *wanted* to beg her to stay? And only pushed her away and left because he felt such an urgent need to protect her from his father? She knew what that man was capable of. She had kissed the scars on Joaquin's skin.

Was she going to make him beg for her to come back? She should have stayed and showed him love really was a healing force. That it was safe to love her because she would stand by him no matter what.

Oh, God. She had made a terrible mistake.

Joaquin brushed past the tired-looking maid who opened the door of Lorenzo's Madrid town house and walked straight into his father's den.

Lorenzo was in his recliner, holding a cigarette and glass of brandy. He didn't lower the footrest, only squinted at Joaquin through the smoke.

The smell was both pungent and stale. Sickeningly familiar, bringing back too many memories of being called on the carpet for beratement or punishment.

Joaquin refused to think of that now. He was as cold and detached as the man before him.

"I wondered why you were diddling your assistant. Do you really think threats from her family will scare me?"

"They should." Joaquin set his phone next to the ashtray and sat on the chair beside his father's. "You're threatening an innocent woman who has nothing to do with you or me."

"She left you? That's too bad." His father puffed smugly on his cigarette.

A deep, aching emptiness had opened in his chest on his way here. Joaquin had never been so terrified in his life as when he had watched Siobhan flip that man into the water. Then he had seen her pulling away from him because she believed he had betrayed her.

I thought it was safe to love you, but it's not.

When she had said those words, they had lashed the back of his heart in the most painfully sweet way. All of him had stung as he absorbed something that ought to feel foreign. Threatening, even. Instead, his response had borne a strong resemblance to a soft, new tenderness that had been germinating inside him. He had wanted to catch her close and explore that, but no, loving him was not safe.

Until he left his father in a pile of his own ruin, Siobhan would never be safe.

So he had let her go, even though he had thought it might kill him. Even though walking out on her could break all those tiny threads that had begun to bind them together.

This had to be done. This bully would not rest until

his ass was in the dirt and that was where Joaquin would put him, once and for all.

"I want the proceeds off the patent for the relay I designed."

Lorenzo snorted. "Cash running low now you don't have the backing of the Sauveterres?"

Joaquin didn't bother correcting him on his very healthy bank balance. "Would you rather I sued you to prove I'm the rightful owner? That you stole that design from me?"

"Who would believe you? You were a child."

"And yet I did it."

"With the education I paid for."

"And that gave you the right to take it as your own? I have since built up credibility in that field, in case you haven't noticed. Meanwhile, everything you released after my design was a second-rate knockoff of a competitor's design. Have you ever wished you'd kept me around to continue working for LVG?"

"No. I don't like you. I never have." He jabbed his cigarette stub into the pile of them in the ashtray.

"And why is that?" Joaquin asked, so filled with cold hatred, he no longer cared, but he made himself ask, "What did I ever do to you that I deserved to be put in hospital at eleven?"

"You're too much like your mother. Fernando looked like me, at least. You..." Lorenzo curled his lip. "And you never knew your place."

"You disgust me." He really did. Joaquin's stomach was turning. "I should have you up on charges for attempted murder. I was a child."

"A clumsy one." His father lit another cigarette.

"So you claimed. We both know what happened."

"I know that you wouldn't shut up about visiting your mother."

"Why didn't you let me live with her if you hated us both so much?" Joaquin was lancing a boil that had sat in him for too long, simply because he couldn't stand to be in the same room. Tonight, however, he would get the answers he needed, no matter how unpleasant or painful.

"Because that's what she wanted," his father said with a cruel curl of his lip. "And so did you."

"You put me in the hospital so I couldn't go to her. And refused to let her visit."

"It shut you up, didn't it?"

"Do you revel in making people suffer? Is that it?"

"I like to win. It's not my fault you've always been too weak to fight back."

"I was a child," he scoffed. "And I've never seen decency as a weakness. Another way I was like my mother, I suppose." He twisted his lips with contempt. "But you're right. I've always deluded myself into believing I could reason with you, but that's not possible, is it? I thought cutting you from my life would be enough, but you can't stand that I have succeeded in spite of you. In spite of your *theft*."

"That really sticks in your craw, doesn't it? Fine. I'll trade the proceeds on what remains of the patent in exchange for your shares in LVG."

"There are only a few years left on the patent. No. Go back to when I handed you the drawing and I'll consider it, since that's when the real money was made."

"It doesn't matter that you designed it. *I* funded the development of it."

"LVG funded the development. Which is why I'm keeping the company, by the way."

"I'll burn it to the ground before I let you keep it."

"Arson?" Joaquin rose and picked up his phone. "This is a useless conversation. As usual."

"See?" His father lowered the footrest and hitched forward on his chair. "This is why I treated you the way I did. It's so easy to best you. You never fight back. You don't *deserve* to be my son and have what I have. You give in too easily."

"I don't want to be your son. And I haven't given in." Joaquin glanced up from tapping the screen on his phone. He waited until the whooshing sound confirmed the file had sent. "I'm playing your game. Doing whatever it takes. You lie and cheat and threaten and steal. So that's what I've done." He tilted his phone. "Our conversation is with my lawyer. You'll be hearing from him on the stolen patent and the attempted murder that you just confessed to. And the arson you've threatened."

Lorenzo made a scoffing noise and threw his head back, but his gaze followed the phone as Joaquin pushed it back into his pocket.

"How does it feel? Never mind. I don't care," Joaquin derided. "Your debts are being called. By me. You might hang on to this house, but you'll lose everything in it. I've also decided to claim the artwork that was Mother's. Her will stated one third to her spouse, two-thirds to her children. You didn't know I knew that, did you?" He hadn't wanted the hassle of going after it, but all bets were off now.

"I've put a lien on the yacht until the audit at LVG completes. There are a lot of unanswered questions around misappropriation of funds." He started to leave then turned back. "The woman you keep in the pied-a-terre in Paris? She's been informed that the money tree has been cut down. She'll be gone by morning with whatever you might have squirreled in the safe there."

Lorenzo was turning purple, eyes sparking with outrage, but all Joaquin could think was how pathetic he looked.

"I'm not throwing you into the street the way you did me. Not because I'm too weak to do it, but because I don't need to. You'll be there soon enough." He started for the door.

The ashtray struck the wall beside the door, puffing ashes across Joaquin's sleeve.

"You're losing your aim, old man. I'm having restraining orders prepared. Zurina, the children, Siobhan. *Me*. We're all off-limits. Never speak to any of us again."

He walked out.

It was dawn on the first day of the New Year when Joaquin entered his empty penthouse in Barcelona.

He was exhausted, but he didn't stop to sleep. He only confirmed that Siobhan had actually left him, retrieved a box from the safe, then headed back to the airport.

He had the sense to check the security log before he filed his flight plan and learned Siobhan hadn't flown to Marbella as he'd thought. She had gone north, to London, so that was where he told the pilot to aim his plane.

It should have been a straight shot. New Year's Day was a slow day for travel. Half the world was sleeping off their celebrations from the night before, but a freak snowstorm over France forced his plane to land at the private airfield in Paris.

Swearing wearily, he disembarked and had the concierge book him into the onsite hotel. It catered to traveling VIPs like himself so his luggage was handled for him and his room details were sent to his phone. He would catch a few winks until the skies cleared then finish his trip.

As he walked into the lobby, he texted Siobhan.

I'm on my way to London to see you.

No. Don't come, she replied.

He stopped in his tracks, immediately swamped by grief. Not the grief that accompanied death, like Fernando. Not the loss of something taken, either. It was the loss of giving up something within himself, making himself vulnerable. Making his needs known. It was the grief of offering himself and knowing he would never be whole again because a piece of himself was hers now.

And she didn't want him. He was being discarded.

His phone pinged. He almost didn't look at it. It was all he could do to stay on his feet.

I'm on my way back, her text read.

To him?

For one second, he experienced that old feeling of desire. The one he tempered out of fear. What if he only lost her again a different way?

Hell, he might, he realized.

Don't go to Barcelona, he quickly texted. I'm grounded in Paris.

In the same second that he heard a distant ping, he heard a feminine voice say a confused, "What?" It came from around the corner. "So am I," she murmured. "Where in Paris?"

He took three long steps forward. His phone dinged in his hand, but he didn't have to read the message because there she was, standing in front of the elevators, staring at her phone. She wore a pink puffer jacket and jeans stuffed into boots rimmed in faux fur. Her hair was sparkling where snowflakes had landed and melted.

"Are you at Charles de Gaulle?" he asked her, voice rasped by disbelief.

She picked up her head and her eyes welled as she stared at him. Her lips began to quiver and her voice hitched. "No. I'm here."

He walked forward and snatched her into his arms.

They kissed forever. Hard enough to hurt, but it was a good hurt. It was the kind of hurt that uncramped muscle and knitted bone. It was the hurt of thawed flesh warming and prickling back to life.

It was the agony of apology and remorse and forgiveness.

"Um. Excuse me?"

They broke apart to see the doors had opened and a pair of well-dressed older women were trying to step out.

"We have a flight," one said.

"Of course." Joaquin steadied Siobhan as they stepped out of the way, then they both stepped into the empty elevator. "Have you been to your room? Come to mine."

"Heard that before," she said under her breath, then gave him a helpless, befuddled look. "I can't believe we're both *here*."

"No? I'm not surprised."

Fate? Did he really believe that?

He took her hand and led her to the room he'd been assigned, using his phone to access it then pulling her inside.

"I would have chosen to ground you here if I'd thought you'd be in the air. Were you really coming back to me?" He trapped her against the door. "Are you okay?" He ran his hands over her beneath her open coat, sparking need within her to be close, close, close. "Is the baby okay?"

"We're both fine. And yes. I just..." She cupped his face and brought his mouth back to hers. "Can we—?"

"Yes." He pushed her jacket off her shoulders and they stripped on their way to the bed.

Was it the most tender, prolonged lovemaking in history? Not at all. It bordered on frantic and stung a little because she wasn't quite ready, but she needed this connection *now*.

She gasped and he froze.

"Hurt?" He cupped her jaw and started to withdraw.

"No. Stay." She wrapped arms and legs around him. The sands in the hourglass stopped falling. Time itself halted as she kneaded her fingers into his hair and skimmed her thighs over his flanks and scraped her teeth against his whiskered chin.

"I shouldn't have left you like that," he groaned, burying his mouth in her throat.

"Shh. I don't want to talk about him. I just want to feel you."

"But I should have said it back, Siobhan. I love you. I love you so much…" His eyes misted. "Saying it aloud felt too dangerous. You wouldn't have left and I was scared for you. You are very, very precious to me, *mi amor*." He traced her eyebrow and followed an invisible line to the corner of her mouth. "You're everything I want. You've become someone I *need. You.* I don't know how to make you believe that."

"I do believe you," she said, letting the glow of it seep into the old fractures in her heart and heal them. Letting herself feel his love as the acceptance and celebration of her that it was. "I love you, too."

She set about making sure he felt it, just as he imbued every kiss and caress with tenderness and worship. They sighed and whispered endearments and groaned with sweet torture. The feelings intensified as they ascended toward a heavenly peak, until they were both caught there, clinging and sweaty and joyous. Drunk on each other. On love.

"I want to stay here forever," she gasped.

"We will," he said. Then held her tight as they fell.

They did what they had wanted to do in San Francisco. They stayed in bed, dozing between making love and ordering food.

Their luggage turned up eventually, not that they used more than a toothbrush.

"Should we go into the city?" he asked at one point.

"Cinnia would give me the code for their penthouse. It overlooks the Eiffel Tower."

It was already dark and they were comfortable in bed so they turned on a movie and fell asleep before it was finished.

She woke to find Joaquin wearing a frown as he read his phone.

"What's wrong?" she asked.

"Killian wanted me to know my father is catching a flight to Saint Lucia. They don't extradite to Spain."

"Will you have him stopped?"

"No." He had told her about his conversation with his father. "As evidence goes, his confession was incriminating, but it still would mean years in court. That's why I didn't try something like it sooner. That, and I didn't want to sink to his level."

She shifted so she could see the scar on his ribs and bent to set a kiss there. "Do you want to tell me about that?"

"Do you really love me?" He tucked his hand at the side of her neck, expression grave.

She was shocked and a little hurt that he would question it. "With my whole heart."

"Then no. I don't want to tell you. It will hurt you. I don't want to do that."

And somehow, that hurt more. Because it was a kindness at his own expense.

She pressed herself half over him, pulling him under

the shelter of her slender arm and leg, wanting to cry for him. For the boy he'd been.

"The one thing I have never wanted to be is like him." He stroked her hair as he spoke. "But there was no other way to deal with him except to double-cross him. It felt wrong to do it. It's not the sort of person I want to be, but when he caused you to be attacked, I wanted to kill him. I really did. That is not the sort of husband and father you and the baby need. The kind you deserve. I questioned whether I should come after you."

She picked up her head, alarmed. "What changed your mind?"

"I thought of Fernando," he said simply. "He was equally cold-blooded when he took over at LVG after Lorenzo's heart attack. It was underhanded, the way he moved with the board to unseat him, but he had to do it. And he bore the consequences for years." He ran his thumb over her bottom lip. "Zurina still loved him. Which gave me hope that you would love me, too."

She ran her teeth across the tingle he'd left in her lip. "I wasn't sure if you loved me, but I thought you might, if I gave you a chance."

"Of course, I love you. It sits like a beacon inside me. That's what scared me. I had trained myself not to hope. I tried to hold back from you, but it's there all the same. Hope and want and a craving for you like I crave air. Maybe you're right. Maybe fate does want us to be together, but I need you to know that I'm *choosing* you, Siobhan. I'm choosing to love. To believe I can have you in my life. I'm doing this badly." He scraped his hand over his face.

"No. You're doing it right." She spilled her naked body over his. Her own chest full of hope and joy and gleaming love.

"Okay, then. Will you... Wait one sec." He rolled her off him and stretched to reach the sleeve of his coat, dragging it from the chair to the bed. He fished through the pockets. "Will you wear this?" He opened the ring box to reveal a square diamond on a split band encrusted with smaller diamonds. It sparkled and shot prisms into the backs of her eyes, dazzling her.

"Are you asking me to marry you?" A smile was taking over her whole face.

"Because I love you, yes. Because I can't imagine my life without you. Because we're having a baby and I want to give you the family that you long for."

Oh. She blinked away fresh, emotive tears.

"Well." She cleared her throat. "Since it would be very comfortable and convenient to have the person I love and want to make babies with be my husband, I accept." She held her finger for him to put it on her.

"Brat." He brought her hand to his lips and kissed her fingertips. "Never leave me again. That was among the worst moments of my life."

"I never will," she promised with a press of her quivering lips to his.

EPILOGUE

One year later...

IT WAS THEIR wedding day. They were keeping it small, family only, and marrying at *Sus Brazos*. Siobhan's mother and sisters were here along with Zurina and her children and, of course, all the Sauveterres and their children.

It was the delightful madhouse of her dreams.

Siobhan should already be on her way to the suite that had been set aside for primping and setting hair and dressing her in her simple, seed-pearl encrusted gown.

Her groom had his own places to be, but he hadn't left their rooms yet, either. They had slept together last night and made love this morning.

A few minutes ago, Siobhan had finished feeding Rogelio, their four-month-old son. Joaquin had lingered instead of leaving, then took Rogelio while Siobhan stepped into the shower.

Along with nannies, there was a grandmother and countless aunties dying to hold him. All the other children wanted a turn giving him a cuddle and having photos with him, but as Siobhan came out of the bathroom in her robe, she found Rogelio was still here, playing with his father.

Joaquin sat in the armchair with Rogelio clasped in one arm. Rogelio was still in his jammies. He was strengthening his wobbly legs against Joaquin's thigh, one hand curled into the soft T-shirt Joaquin wore.

He chewed his fist as he watched the small teddy bear that Joaquin slowly swooped toward him. "He's going to tickle your belly."

As the plush bear arrived in Rogelio's middle, the baby let out infectious baby chortles. Joaquin laughed right along with him.

"Now he's going to get your neck."

Siobhan stood struck with wonder as she watched them. It wasn't the first time she'd seen Joaquin be so tender with their son. It happened many times a day, but it filled her with awe and tenderness and pure happiness every time. In this moment, the sight of Joaquin's defenses completely down as he allowed his naked love for his son to shine in his face, brought a squeeze of adoration to her chest and made her eyes sting with joy.

He noticed her. "You're ready to go up with him? I'm sorry, little man. If the adoration of all those women gets to be too much, call me and I'll take you to the barber with me." Joaquin dropped the teddy bear so he could pinch a lock of fine strands in two fingers to measure it. "You could use a shave and a cut, no? While we talk politics and the economy?"

"Do you want to take him to the barber with you?" Siobhan asked with amusement.

"I do." Joaquin looked at their son's big blinking eyes

and swiped his thumb beneath his drooling mouth. "But your family will be disappointed if I take him so I will share him."

Rogelio caught his finger and brought his knuckle to his mouth, using it as a teething toy, then kicked with excitement when she came close enough to reach for him.

"We'll have him to ourselves on the honeymoon," she reminded Joaquin as she took the baby and he rose to kiss her.

His wide hand splayed itself on her ass through the thin silk of her robe. "I'm looking forward to having *you* to myself on the honeymoon," he said in a low, sexy voice.

"Then we should get married, shouldn't we?"

"Details, details," he chided, cupping their son's head to press a kiss to his temple, then kissing her once more. "I'll see you soon."

A few hours later, Henri escorted Siobhan down the aisle to where Joaquin waited for her. Zurina stood up for him in Fernando's place. Cinnia was Siobhan's matron of honor. She held Rogelio, their ring bearer in an adorable baby tuxedo.

Siobhan teared up as they spoke their vows and pure love radiated from Joaquin's eyes. Her voice shook with emotion as she devoted herself to him, and he promised himself to her.

Later, after photographs and speeches, a song performed by the chorus of children and a wonderful dinner, Joaquin took her into his arms for their first dance.

Siobhan had requested "At Last", but for some reason, the band began to sing about Paris and Rome.

As wedding glitches went, it was nothing so Siobhan didn't make a fuss. The song was pretty and danceable. It seemed familiar, but Siobhan didn't place it until the crooner lamented that he had left his heart in San Francisco.

"Did you do this?" she asked, tilting her head back with amusement.

"What?"

"Change the song?"

"Is this not the song you wanted?" He was wearing a relaxed expression, not the one that hid his thoughts. He wasn't laughing at her and only looked mildly curious as he met her gaze.

"You're teasing me," she accused. "*This* song?"

"I didn't do anything. I swear. Do you not like it? It seems appropriate." His mouth twitched wryly at the lyrics.

"You really didn't ask them to sing this?"

"I really didn't." He touched his mouth to hers. "It must be kismet."

It must have been.

* * * * *

Did you fall head over heels for
Boss's Christmas Baby Acquisition?

*Then be sure to check out
these other dazzling stories
from Dani Collins!*

Husband for the Holidays
His Highness's Hidden Heir
Maid to Marry
Hidden Heir, Italian Wife
The Greek's Wife Returns

*And catch up with the rest of the
Sauveterre siblings in:*

Pursued by the Desert Prince
His Mistress with Two Secrets
Bound by the Millionaire's Ring
Prince's Son of Scandal

Available now!

Get up to 4 Free Books!

We'll send you 2 free books from each series you try PLUS a free Mystery Gift.

FREE Value Over **$25**

Both the **Harlequin Presents** and **Harlequin Medical Romance** series feature exciting stories of passion and drama.

YES! Please send me 2 FREE novels from Harlequin Presents or Harlequin Medical Romance and my FREE gift (gift is worth about $10 retail). After receiving them, if I don't wish to receive any more books, I can return the shipping statement marked "cancel." If I don't cancel, I will receive 6 brand-new larger-print novels every month and be billed just $7.19 each in the U.S. or $7.99 each in Canada, or 4 brand-new Harlequin Medical Romance Larger-Print books every month and be billed just $7.19 each in the U.S. or $7.99 each in Canada, a savings of 20% off the cover price. It's quite a bargain! Shipping and handling is just 50¢ per book in the U.S. and $1.25 per book in Canada.* I understand that accepting the 2 free books and gift places me under no obligation to buy anything. I can always return a shipment and cancel at any time. The free books and gift are mine to keep no matter what I decide.

Choose one: ☐ **Harlequin Presents Larger-Print** (176/376 BPA G36Y)   ☐ **Harlequin Medical Romance** (171/371 BPA G36Y)   ☐ **Or Try Both!** (176/376 & 171/371 BPA G36Z)

Name (please print)

Address   Apt. #

City   State/Province   Zip/Postal Code

Email: Please check this box ☐ if you would like to receive newsletters and promotional emails from Harlequin Enterprises ULC and its affiliates. You can unsubscribe anytime.

Mail to the **Harlequin Reader Service:**
IN U.S.A.: P.O. Box 1341, Buffalo, NY 14240-8531
IN CANADA: P.O. Box 603, Fort Erie, Ontario L2A 5X3

Want to explore our other series or interested in ebooks? Visit www.ReaderService.com or call 1-800-873-8635.

---

*Terms and prices subject to change without notice. Prices do not include sales taxes, which will be charged (if applicable) based on your state or country of residence. Canadian residents will be charged applicable taxes. Offer not valid in Quebec. This offer is limited to one order per household. Books received may not be as shown. Not valid for current subscribers to the Harlequin Presents or Harlequin Medical Romance series. All orders subject to approval. Credit or debit balances in a customer's account(s) may be offset by any other outstanding balance owed by or to the customer. Please allow 4 to 6 weeks for delivery. Offer available while quantities last.

Your Privacy—Your information is being collected by Harlequin Enterprises ULC, operating as Harlequin Reader Service. For a complete summary of the information we collect, how we use this information and to whom it is disclosed, please visit our privacy notice located at https://corporate.harlequin.com/privacy-notice. Notice to California Residents – Under California law, you have specific rights to control and access your data. For more information on these rights and how to exercise them, visit https://corporate.harlequin.com/california-privacy. For additional information for residents of other U.S. states that provide their residents with certain rights with respect to personal data, visit https://corporate.harlequin.com/other-state-residents-privacy-rights/.

HPHM25